PRAISE FOR ASCENDESCENSCION, THE PROCESS IS LOVE

"This is a great set of stories! Each story has a satisfying trajectory and I felt like I got to know each of the characters' motivations and personalities even within the constraints of a short story. I also enjoyed the deeper themes throughout Ascendescenscion. I loved the thought-provoking concepts raised throughout the book. These points were especially great in combination with the occasional instance of humor. Overall, it was a fun read!" - Reader Review

"I have read the author's other works and I have to say, E. S. Fein is really impressing me! The authors main novel 'Points of Origin' was a wonderful journey exploring consciousness and self, and here we once again have an exploration of existence, but the density of it all is very neatly packed into four riveting short stories. Characters experience growth, show a curiosity of the unknowable, and explore new interesting subject matter. Every story has left me lost in thought and filled with questions, which is exactly what I hope for when I read good Sci Fi. Excited to see where E. S. Fein will take us next!!!" - Reader Review

"... Gave me chills... an ayahuasca trip dipped in DMT... awesome stories!" - MR, EnticeYourMind.com

"Beautiful, profound, eerie, bizarre -- E. S. Fein's collection of short stories explores the concept and execution of love_using settings that seem at first completely devoid of any such feeling, however, the true nature of each tale is masterfully_revealed with each line of flowing prose. Mind-leeching AI, flesh-eating storm systems, sentient singularities, and_machines more passionate than their human counterparts converge in this science fiction anthology that is partly a_transhumanist anthem and partly a declaration that no matter how strange or bleak things get, love will somehow always_remain the driving force. Five out of five stars!" - Reader Review

OTHER WORKS BY E. S. FEIN

A Dream of Waking Life
Points of Origin
The Process is Love

OfficialESFein.com
Instagram.com/AuthorESFein
Patreon.com/OfficialESFein
Facebook.com/AuthorESFein

ASCENDESCENSCION/ THE PROCESS IS LOVE

Two Short Story Collections

E. S. Fein

Ascendescenscion/The Process is Love

Author E. S. Fein

Publisher: Feinbooks

Editor: Nichole Paolella Petrovich

Illustrator: Leraynne

ISBN: 978-1-7323069-5-0

June 2022

First Edition

THANK YOU

to Moi and Pop, for your endless lessons…

to Melissa and Dave, for your ceaseless support...

to Marcin and Maggie, for your friendship...

to Jesse, for inspiring me to always improve…

to Rachel, for your invaluable critiques...

to Claire, for believing my tales to be worthwhile stories...

to Nichole, for transforming my stories into worthwhile fantasies…

to Mom, for listening to me spin fantasies into tales for as long as I could speak...

CONTENTS

ASCENDESCENSCION

THE PROCESS IS LOVE

ASCENDESCENSCION

A Short Story Collection

Multiversal Beauty

Luscious curls meticulously straightened to straw-like strands; stiletto heels and the damn dangly belly button ring; her lipstick, the pink one called Modest (which Dan had once referred to as the hot color) liberally applied. Something about too much lipstick always used to turn him on.

She strode into the den, breathing heavily to work her skin into a soft blush. The lingerie felt uncomfortably tight–a foreign relic of their youth. The holoscreen flooded Dan's eyes with younger, prettier, better women wearing heaps of lipstick and tailored to Dan's fantasies and probably his deeply hidden fetishes when Jessica wasn't home.

"Danny?" Jessica purred. But her soft, sultry voice couldn't contend with the boob-bouncing action of Dan's favorite custom show: Blade Babes.

"Dan!"

Dan barely lifted an arm to shoo her away. "Not now, babe. Judy's fighting Monica, Goddess of the barbarianesses."

"Daniel Colley!" Jessica shrieked, shaking and unable to contain herself.

He finally gave her a full two seconds attention, glancing at her thighs and breasts as if to assess them relative to his precious bikini babes.

"What?" Dan asked simply, then turned back to the breast-jiggling.

"Nothing, Dan. It's nothing."

"Okay, honey."

Okay. That's all Dan could muster despite Jessica literally fawning. It'd been three years since they last had sex. So maybe she was flabbier than the bikini babes. It's not like Dan was a prize anymore either. Plus, after thirty years together, things were bound to get stale. But this was just ridiculous. He made her feel like a mere part of the environment…and not for the first time.

"I'm not a fucking bookshelf, Dan!"

"Okay, honey," Dan issued with a half-hearted shoo.

Jessica dressed herself, removed the make up, then left for the lab without saying goodbye.

"Fuck him," Jessica assured herself as Q-lab's access terminal scanned her retina. The laboratory doors opened to an array of humming machinery that Jessica had built herself. That's exactly why she had no qualms using it, despite it technically being government property. *You're a quantum physicist*, Jessica told herself. *One of the few in the world. And Dan's a fucking car mechanic.*

Jessica donned the neural headset. She wished she wasn't still attracted to him. She could probably have anyone from any universe at any time if she really wanted. Yet somehow, even when she was a young PhD student, all she could ever think about was Dan.

She let out a long sigh, cursing herself for caring about him. *But people can't choose their attractions.*

"I wish Dan loved me for who I am…No! I wish Dan saw me as a queen…NO! A goddess–the goddess of every universe and multiverse."

The machinery moaned, processing her words and rewriting the multiversal continuum. She felt a twinge of guilt using the quantum terminal for such a selfish reason, but the lab would have to do a test run at some point anyway. She was doing the world a favor, and soon enough humanity would be capable of rewriting reality in any way it dreamed. For now though, she would test it on Dan. What would he care anyway? He'd still have his bikini babes.

She removed the headset.

"Queen Jessica," came a soft baritone from behind her. "Is it really you, Divine One?"

Jessica turned to find a doorway of light shrinking into nothingness. In front of the doorway knelt an oversized man clad in ultra-futuristic, diamond armor. He bowed his head so the only unarmored part of him, his face, was left unseen. A gleaming broadsword hung from his back and emitted a bright, rainbow brilliance. The polished armor glowed with a supernatural aura, and much of it was adorned with emblems and writing. The armor plating of his shoulders, each like a boulder more massive than a whole man, was engraved with a pulsing maroon that read: "For the Queen."

"Who…" Jessica managed.

The armored man lifted his face and smiled gallantly. It was Dan.

"I've traversed the quantum folds opened by your machine, my Queen. For a subjective thousand years I have slain every form of wickedness and waded through every entangled, multiversal labyrinth across countless universes to find you."

The knight's jawline was sharper than her Dan's, and there was no doubt his body was chiseled from something even more Herculean than his divinely glowing armor.

"You are Queen. You are Goddess. Jessica, the Multiversal Beauty."

He reached out a gauntlet of shimmering diamond. "Would you take my hand, and–"

A blade of black smoke suddenly protruded from his mouth, then retracted just as quickly through his brain and skull. He fell, a pile of diamond, and another Dan clothed in swimming, ebony shadows stood before her now.

She wanted to scream, but her shock was too great.

"He was weak, Goddess. I am your loyal servant," the shadow armored Dan proclaimed.

Another doorway opened, and this time a humanoid-machine emerged, with steel face and red, glowing eyes. The shape and structure of the face was unmistakable.

"Dans of the flesh are mortal and thus unfit to serve you, Goddess," the machine intoned before vaporizing the shadow Dan with a pulse of its eyes. The machine knelt before Jessica, ignoring the dead, diamond armored Dan. Before the machine could pledge its undying fealty, a rain of luminous, particulate matter poured into the room from multiple locations and ground the machine Dan to dust.

Trembling panic bubbled through Jessica.

The room vibrated with the voice of the light particles. "Dans requiring a solid form are not fit to be servants of Goddess Jessica."

More doorways were opening. Jessica sprung to pick up the neural headset, but the diamond armored Dan had crushed it in his dying collapse.

The particles of light vanished, replaced by a bodiless, spectral voice. Something beyond matter and energy sang with an angelic pitch reminiscent of Dan's lilt and tone. "Goddess Jessica, surely Dans requiring atomic structure and bound by the Planck limit can never truly be fit to serve you."

Jessica stood frozen.

The voice was strangled into nothingness by something even stranger. Still, more doorways opened.

Her Patient, Pleasant Proboscis

As an eighteen-year-old university graduate, Billy Covey prided himself on being the youngest paid employee in the history of Genomic Mapping Services (GMS)–known worldwide as the CERN of molecular genetics. Most scientists only dreamed of walking inside its illustrious halls rather than lurking bitterly outside its exterior as they mucked through existential quicksand. Hordes of amateur intellects would regularly peer through windows from a distance, hoping futilely for a glimpse at genetic Wonderland. Billy was no longer surprised by the balding, middle-aged dudes and the occasional well-dressed woman in her fifties stalking the building in a fever dream of lost hope. In fact, Billy often goaded them, waving and smiling as they sauntered past on their way to some lesser building and lesser living. Billy was inside, and they were outside. That's what made being an employee of GMS so prestigious, even glorious. It meant Billy was part of the elite, and because he was the youngest and thus filled with the greatest potential, he found it easy to think of himself as the elite of the elite.

Simply put, Billy Covey was certain he would do great things. He already knew, of course, what his magnum opus would be: the cause of more human disease than any other organism; the supplier of human anguish on a global scale; the vampiric dealer of death.

The mosquito.

Billy would soon be master of the mosquito. Every single one would be under his control, and the world would never be the same in Billy's wake.

Billy allowed his mind a moment to daydream before returning to the holographic display of the microscope's field of view. A hyper-focused view of Billy's custom-made synthetic exon was set against a background of the mosquito's entire genetic map. The exon, to which he had devoted every waking and dreaming moment of his free and professional time, set the dark room aflame with red, blue, green, and white LEDs, illuminating each of the exon's nitrogenous bases like torches lighting the way to humanity's future. Billy was the torch bearer.

He smirked and conjured a vision of himself surrounded by the fresh, healthy people of his new world as angelic mosquitoes dove to administer cures and remedies and biological transformations to every living person in need of his help. He was their savior, their messiah, their God even. Billy chuckled pleasantly to himself and reeled back the tail end of the vision. Savior was more than enough. He'd save Godhood for another time–maybe after a few more world-transforming experiments.

"Billy!" someone crowed from behind the office door.

Billy rolled his eyes. It was probably a colleague asking his advice, or worse, it was some petty, time-wasting demand cast from up-high.

"Come in," Billy sighed, waving away the projection and illuminating the room.

The door opened, blasting Billy's still-readjusting eyes with a spray of intrusive, penetrating photons. Billy groaned at the sight of Dr. Havenshaw, his original recruiter. This could mean only one thing: a pain in the ass.

"What?" Billy asked indignantly.

Dr. Havenshaw curled his lips in disappointment, maybe even disdain at some level, and thrust an accusing finger at Billy.

"You're done, Covey."

Billy didn't hold back his laughter. They wouldn't rid themselves of their child prodigy–no way they would.

"You've said that before, Doctor," Billy reminded him without an ounce of concern.

Doctor Havenshaw capitulated with a nod, then said, "you're right. But this is the final straw. I told you we'd be keeping an eye on you, and I've kept my word."

"Meaning?"

"We've spent far too many resources on you, Billy. You're smart. I'll give you that."

"Can I get back to work, Doctor?" Billy droned.

Doctor Havenshaw's knees began shaking, stifling an outburst. He thrust his finger harder at Billy and inched a few steps closer to him.

"I trusted you, Billy. I thought you were mature enough for this job. Now it's my ass. We know you've done nothing these past two months except work on your damn mosquito-god gene–"

"Mosquito-commander," Billy corrected, though he liked the sound of Doctor Havenshaw's suggested title. Commander and God of trillions of tiny lives, eventually quintillions and more. A self-replenishing bank of mobile medicine and custom-cures. He could already see genetic code growing outward from the synthetic exon, complex fractals of atomic structure built for the single purpose of bolstering humanity into what it was always intended to be, into–

"I don't care what you're calling that nonsense!" Havenshaw barked unexpectedly. "We don't have a contract for mosquitoes, Billy. Tomatoes. Fucking tomatoes. Corn. Wheat. Fucking pumpkins–I don't care. Not your damn mosquitoes!"

Billy couldn't believe he had genuinely forgotten that GMS worked solely with food crops. It just didn't seem to matter compared to the mosquito-commander gene and the new world, a world where food and sustenance in general would seem barbaric, even savage.

"Are you even listening, Billy?"

"Food…yeah…I get it."

"You don't!"

Billy waited for Doctor Havenshaw to continue, but he wasn't budging.

"Can I get back to work, Doctor?"

The messianic dream beckoned Billy to complete his work before even a single further person suffered needlessly.

"Billy!" Doctor Havenshaw scowled. "It's over, Billy. We have days of video evidence showing complete and utter neglect for your work. This isn't your personal lab, and the world isn't your personal plaything. One of these days you're going to do something you'll regret, Billy. You're out of control."

Doctor Havenshaw's words barely registered. Each of these moments was but a forgettable instance of exposition in the new story Billy was writing for humanity.

Billy didn't need GMS. He didn't need Havenshaw. He didn't need anyone–except the mosquitoes.

"Are you done, Doctor?"

Havenshaw shook his head, reading Billy for some sign that he fully comprehended he wouldn't be allowed back to work at GMS the next day or any other day thereafter. He'd be like the scientists outside: a nobody.

"You have an hour to pack up your things, Billy. You'll be inspected upon exit to ensure you don't have any GMS property on your person. Good luck out there, Billy. Try not to fuck over another recruiter, okay?"

Billy offered a shallow nod to Doctor Havenshaw.

"Good luck, Billy," Havenshaw repeated before leaving Billy's office with a disappointed skulk.

Billy smiled with voracious, prophetic delight. He had one hour…more than enough time.

The North was lost. The South had fallen almost immediately. The East and West were a permanent black-as-night ebony buzzing across the landscape of John's childhood. Death covered the whole surface of the Earth, marrying and multiplying itself to fill even the furthest reaches of the planet's atmosphere–maybe even beyond. The underground bunkers–humanity's final strongholds–were all that remained, though John could easily envision the sqeets teaching themselves to spelunk and bore into bunkers as easily as termites converting dead wood into sustenance.

"You alright, John?"

John almost jumped out of his skin. He had lost himself in the doom written across the face of the electronic map in front of him.

It showed endless black without any detail whatsoever–an all-consuming void of buzzing death.

"You scared the hell out of me, Jen," John chuckled. "I was..." John almost lost himself in his thoughts again.

"Planning?" Jennifer offered.

The suggestion was good enough.

"Something like that," John answered. His mind prodded him with crying visions of himself and the other eight occupants of Bunker-28 being ripped from their warm flesh by sqeets the size of cars, some of them even busses. Now, there was a thought worth savoring – not the death part, but the feeling of riding down the open road in his iris blue '99 Porsche 996 with Jennifer by his side. He could almost see her now, her loose tank top falling from one shoulder as the wind cascaded through her hair, painting the sky behind her with twirling blonde tendrils. He imagined them on an endless road to nowhere, just driving away, anywhere beyond the reach of the sqeets. John knew, of course, that there was no such location outside the miniscule human pockets dotting the face of the Earth like a littering of unnatural follicles. It was only a matter of time before the sqeets uprooted even the bunkers, solidifying humanity's extinction.

John pulled himself out from beneath the onslaught of his doom-thoughts. He needed to keep his head straight. For the others...and most of all for Jennifer.

"Food rations. How's Bunker-30 handling rations? Are you guys still in surplus?" John asked, searching for some pragmatic thought to anchor his mind.

"Yes," Jennifer confirmed with a static hiss. "Our rations remain consistent. All is well here, John."

John felt the sudden need to hold Jen. He hadn't felt her freckled, alabaster skin against his in just over 19 months, and during that time over one thousand miles of rock, air, and sqeets kept them apart.

"Jen," John gasped.

"What is it, John?" Jennifer asked, worry filling her voice.

John cursed the bunker for not being equipped with visual transmission. If only he could see her...

"I miss you, Jennifer."

"John..."

"I miss you."

"Signing off, Sergeant."

Jennifer severed the connection on her end, but John kept the line open. Sentiment like that was too much for her, and John knew that. He shouldn't have told her he missed her. It would hurt her infinitely more than what he was feeling. But it was too much–both of them trapped inside coffins, John beneath Chicago and Jennifer beneath Winnipeg. One more day and she would have been on her way home to Chicago. One more day, but Covey couldn't wait another day–that fucking monster. John would never see Jennifer again because of Billy Covey — some random scientist that had barely even finished puberty by the time his work literally consumed him and everyone else in turn.

"Yo, Sergeant."

John almost jumped out of his skin again. He turned to see Private Rodrigo, as unwashed and unkempt as everyone else inside the bunker. Rodrigo kept his distance from John, refusing to even step foot inside the control room.

"Private?"

"Slociak needs to see you, Sergeant," Rodrigo said, his eyes wide in seeming fear at...was it John he was afraid of? Nonsense.

John's mind fluttered with lists of potential problems–all menial and forgettable when paired against the ocean of death above them growing in density and volume with exponentially increasing acceleration. Would the very foundations of the Earth's crust buckle beneath the ceaselessly increasing mass of the sqeets? Would they destroy themselves before they destroyed humanity?

"Sir?" Rodrigo offered, breaking John from more doom-thoughts.

"Yes, Private. I heard you. Lead the way."

Rodrigo didn't bother with an affirmative; he just about-faced and made his way back to one of the bunker's outer rooms. John realized suddenly that it had been weeks, maybe even months, since he had visited these sections of the bunker. After a dozen steps, it was clear they were heading to the grow rooms–cavernous hollows filled with numerous shelves of aquaponics, hydroponics and LED grow lights. The grow rooms in each bunker were designed to remain in surplus indefinitely, recycling every particle of excrement deposited by the bunker's occupants and growing it all back into beans, legumes, fruits, vegetables, seeds–even small tilapia, though only enough to eat on a bi-monthly basis.

John stopped suddenly. There was a familiar, pungent smell in the air.

"What is that, Rodrigo?"

Rodrigo couldn't help a slight smirk. "What me and my boys used to call good shit, Sergeant."

John blinked stupidly.

"Mota, Sergeant. You know–the marijuana."

John shook his head, not sure if this was some prank hatched up by bored privates.

"What the hell are you talking about, Rodrigo?"

Rodrigo nodded slowly and let his smirk fall away, evidently aware of how crazy he sounded.

"Right this way, Sergeant."

John followed Rodrigo through the heavy plastic doorway and shielded his eyes against the LEDs until he had time to adjust. The whole crew was inside the relatively spacious grow room, all of them standing shoulder to shoulder, passing around a small, smoldering…joint?

"Are all of you smoking…marijuana?" John managed, fighting his disbelief. His men were clearly out of control, all of them, but a more pressing question was at hand.

"Where the hell did you get it?"

Corporal Slociak, biologist and head of nutrition and excrement management, stepped forward. His head was closely shaved, but he had allowed his beard to grow completely untouched. The man was just a hair shorter than John, but the way he stood made him seem far taller.

"I grew it, John," Corporal Slociak said. He sucked hard on the joint, then passed it to Private Grubeak, medical specialist and quartermaster.

"You too, Private Grubeak?" John asked, surprised that she had succumbed to such careless behavior. She had always seemed the most levelheaded, even more so than John.

Private Grubeak lowered her head. "John…" she said, glancing at Corporal Slociak as if for approval. Slociak nodded at her, then returned his gaze to John.

"I snuck in seeds from the beginning," Slociak explained, "just in case we needed a way to soften our deaths. You should try some, John. Relax a little, you know?"

The others snickered and turned away from their commander.

"This clearly isn't some harmless prank, as here you all are, getting high on an illegal supply," John reasoned aloud.

The whole crew burst into childish laughter.

"Nice rhyme, Sergeant," Slociak said.

"Shut your mouth, Corporal Slociak," John snapped with the sudden awareness that his soldiers were engaging in mutiny.

"Who…who grew this? Who?"

"I already told you," Slociak winked. "I grew it. To get high."

"How could you do this when–"

"For all of us to get high," Slociak interrupted, "to give our brains a little reprieve 'fore the sqeets suck 'em up like slurpees."

Private Rodrigo lit another joint and passed it to his cousin, Private Himenez. Avoiding eye contact with John, Himenez stole a drag from the joint, then passed it to the normally perfectly disciplined Private Gutierrez.

"That's enough. All of you!" John ordered. The soldiers hesitated for a moment before looking to Slociak for reassurance. In response, Corporal Slociak reached into his front pocket to reveal a third joint, this one even fuller than the first two. He lit it, then offered it to John.

"You're all mad!" John said just loud enough to be heard over the ceaseless humming of water pumps and multi-color LED grow lights.

"You're fucked, John," Slociak told him evenly. "Your mind–I don't blame you, obviously, but all the same, you're–"

"I said enough!" John bellowed with the proper authority of a commander. His face was red and full of nervous perspiration. He hoped the hapless powerlessness he felt inside himself wasn't too thoroughly on display to the others.

"We have a bunker to run. We have people to keep alive," John reminded his crew.

As long as they disposed of the marijuana, discipline and order could be reimplemented. He couldn't blame them for succumbing to weakness with an ocean of bloodthirsty monsters filling the surface of the Earth like an insatiable inferno.

"The survivors of this madness," John continued, "whoever they might be in the distant future, are depending on us to keep discipline. You all know this! You all know how fragile everything is."

Each set of eyes stared at John as if he were already blood-drained sqeet food.

"You've all given up on surviving? Have you given up on humanity itself that easy? You're all giving up just to get high?" John hoped they felt equal shame and disappointment in themselves, but all they offered in exchange for his words were more hollow stares.

"You're totally fucked, John," Slociak stated simply. "You just can't let go."

"No, Corporal," John nearly thrashed at him, "I just don't give up as easily as you. I don't give up, period. You think the other bunkers won't be affected by this news if they ever find out about this? Your actions have very real consequences. What if Jennifer–"

Her name caught in John's throat before he could finish his point.

"Jennifer?" Slociak repeated as the others looked away from John, as if some phantom, unseen pain loomed between them all.

"John..." Slociak considered his words carefully, then gave up on reason and repeated, "you're totally fucked, John. I mean, we're all fucked, but you..."

John strode a single step forward, fully prepared to confiscate and dispose of each and every bit of marijuana he could find.

"Jennifer's dead, John. You know it, too," Slociak said.

John stopped in his tracks.

"Are you that high, Slociak?"

John looked to Rodrigo for support, but the private was busying himself with another fresh joint while pretending to look for something on a nearby shelf.

"John!" Slociak barked. "I am relinquishing your command."

John shook his head. "The hell you are, Corporal Slociak. You're in no shape to command a poodle, let alone a bunker full of lives."

With a nod from Slociak, Rodrigo and Himenez closed the gap, cornering John. Tears filled Grubeak's eyes. Private Wenchek had his back to the others and was visibly shaking. Rodrigo and Himenez grabbed John's arms.

"Get off!" John demanded, attempting to shake the larger men off. His soldiers remained like statues wrapped about his limbs.

"You mutinous bastards! What kind of cheap power play is this, eh Slociak?"

Slociak shook his head with seemingly genuine sorrow. "We can't play along anymore, John. This is the end. No more playing pretend down here. The sqeets will be on us in a matter of days, maybe even hours. Maybe fucking minutes, John. Bunker-29 was taken last week; Bunker-30 was ten days before that. We're next, John. They're purging humanity in descending numerical order– humanity's own numerical order. Like a countdown to our extinction. It's any day now."

"I just talked to Jennifer, you shit-head. She told me the rations are in surplus, and–"

"Only that wasn't really, Jennifer. You loved her. I get it. I get why this is so hard for you."

Slociak wasn't making a bit of sense.

"Then who the fuck do you think I talked to, eh Slociak?" John demanded.

"The sqeets…" Grubeak managed to say with a pathetic crack in her raspy voice. She buried her eyes in her hands and began to silently sob.

"John…you already know all this," Slociak reasoned. "We all listened over the comms as the sqeets broke into her bunker and…and…took her mind over…whatever that means…" Slociak trailed off, imagining his own fate as he forced a final drag out of the now spent joint.

"I just spoke to her–surplus–just spoke to her–she said surplus–she said–" John mumbled to himself, seemingly unaware of the others.

Rodrigo and Himenez brought John to a small bench and sat him down carefully. He was still mumbling to himself when they finally rose to their feet.

"Let the man have a hit," Slociak said, motioning for someone to grab a joint.

Rodrigo tried offering one to John, even placed it directly between his still mumbling lips, but John was too far gone now.

"We…we…we broke…broke his mind completely this time," Grubeak stammered through pitiful sobs.

Slociak pulled hard on a fresh joint.

"Fuck it. He was gone anyway," Slociak reasoned, stifling a sudden pang of raw fear. "And so are we."

"Let's just…let's just enjoy the mota while we still can," Rodrigo said with a fake smile.

"What are we supposed to do with John?"

Slociak considered the question for a few silent moments. John was still mumbling incoherently to himself.

"Put him in the control room. Lock the door. I don't want him doing anything stupid, like snapping back to his old self and actually trying to take the cannabis from us again."

"You think it'll hurt?" Grubeak asked suddenly. "The sqeets, I mean. You guys think it'll hurt when they come for us?"

Slociak shrugged. "Probably." He heaved another drag out of his joint and blew it in John's direction. "Maybe John's the luckiest out of all of us. He won't even know the difference."

"Just talked to her," John muttered. "Just talked to her–surplus–talked to her–Jennifer–"

Something cracked somewhere.

An alarm sounded.

Sirens and flashing red lights warned of a breach somewhere in the hull of the bunker.

Slociak exuded a deep, cannabis-filled sigh. "We already sent what we have to the space station, right?"

"Already done," Rodrigo confirmed, his voice trembling.

"Good," Slociak said simply. The joint between his fingers was nearly ash. He sucked down the last of it, then held his breath for as long as possible.

The sirens stopped all of a sudden.

The room went dark but continued flashing red.

There was an alien movement coming from somewhere, a shifting and shuffling which a human being could never reproduce.

Slociak exhaled into the flashing, crimson silence, wrapping a curling cloud of smoke about the hulking, insectoid bodies standing before them now.

The group of trembling humans took one step back all at once, as if they might constitute a single, terrified entity. The swarm shuffled rhythmically forward, their shimmering proboscises like sharpened straws.

Kito Tanaka watched the Earth.

Every poem and elegant description of the Earth that Kito could think of involved color in some way. Poets and singers of the old world spoke of white, billowing clouds and the life forms below them. They conjured in their art the precise feeling of azure, winding rivers outlined by the dulcet mating rituals of birds. They explored cavern and jungle and ocean and sky. But now it was as if every poem ever written described an alien planet–a spectre of a mythos wrapped in legend and told as tall tale.

The blue Earth, the green Earth, the sandy parts and snowy parts, the lush parts and dead parts–all was forever gone. The Earth was the Swarm, and the Swarm was the Earth. If he didn't know better, if he had not seen the Earth consumed in real time like mold blanketing the soft surface of rotten fruit, then Kito might mistake the planet for a roiling, churning globe of lifeless dark plasma that had always persisted in such a manner since its archaic genesis.

Kito Tanaka watched the Earth.

The Swarm appeared to have reached its maximum growth in altitude six months earlier. The Swarm filled every inch of the visible sky, replacing the world's weather systems with its own swirling array of endless mating and multiplying. This had completely blocked the ISS's bird's-eye view of the Earth's surface, blinding Kito and the others from the details of humanity's extinction. However, all three hundred and forty nine bunkers around the world had continued uploading their multi-spectra data (minus one bunker due to technical malfunctions unrelated to the Swarm). This data provided the ISS with the necessary information needed to construct a visual representation of what exactly was occurring on the surface. The bunkers weren't equipped with sophisticated enough software to represent the same data on their own terminals, meaning they were blind to their own task. They could only send their data and hope it made some type of sense to the eye in the sky.

Kito Tanaka watched the Earth and reminded himself that none of that mattered now. Though the bunkers continued relaying their data, every single bunker had already been systematically breached and scoured. The mind of every human still residing in the bunkers belonged to the Swarm now, whatever that meant. All the while, the Swarm allowed the data to keep being sent, as if they wanted Kito and his crewmates to see what they were doing. And what they were doing defied all logic and understanding of the Swarm, maybe even of life itself.

Kito-kun! Kito-kun! KITO-KUN!

Kito Tanaka issued an unbecoming whimper.

"Enough!" Kito demanded aloud to his mind.

He heard ruffled movement behind him. He'd been careless…desperate to just slip away and let the memories of Her steal his mind away from the present.

Kito-kun!

"What'd you say, Tanaka?" Hemmler asked from inside his velcroed sleeping bag.

"My apologies," Kito bowed with his back to Kyle Hemmler, chief engineer.

"It's nothing," Hemmler yawned. "'Bout time for me to get up anyway."

Hemmler unzipped and stretched in Zero-G like a wriggling worm.

"Ship, let Myra know it's her turn to get some Zs," Hemmler yawned.

Kito knew that Hemmler had barely slept the entire night, tossing and turning in his sleeping bag as his mind wrestled with the inevitable. Kito knew this because it was exactly the same for him and all the others.

"Understood," the station confirmed. It could be heard chiming away in some recess of the makeshift craft that had been patched and repaired a thousand times over. "Annibelle Myra, your three-and-a-half-hour sleep shift will begin in t-minus ten minutes. Please prepare for sleep."

"She's probably plugged in," Hemmler surmised happily. "Let her play, I say. Anything to take our minds off–" Hemmler stopped himself short.

Kito turned and offered him a nod. "You're right, Kyle." Kito realized he hadn't used Hemmler's first name in many months. "I wish video games could occupy my mind like that too. To be honest, I can barely even play. I never had a knack for them, even as a kid."

"We know, Tanaka," Hemmler laughed, likely thinking back to the few times Myra had convinced Kito to play against her in a full-immersion, virtual simulation of surfing on the surface of the sun–its cresting, ultra-luminous plasma a playful environment, albeit dimmed to a fraction of its real-life luminosity.

Kito Tanaka turned back to the viewport and watched the Earth swirl with shapes and patterns and movements that almost perfectly mimicked the endless, plasmic ocean of the Sun's surface.

"How much longer can they possibly last?" Hemmler asked. "I mean, what the hell are they even feeding on at this point? Everything is…"

Not dead. That's what Hemmler couldn't say, for the Earth had never been so dense with life, even if it was a single species that fully dominated the macroscopic biological world.

"This too shall pass, as all things must," Kito intoned.

Kito-kun!

It was Her favorite thing to tell Kito whenever he was in one of his depressive moods.

KITO-KUN!

Kito pinched his nose, attempting to silence Her voice.

"You okay, Tanaka?" Hemmler checked.

"I have a better question," Kito countered, waving off Hemmler's concern. "Where's Myra?"

"She's–" Hemmler turned to see that Myra still hadn't made her way to her sleeping bag.

"Myra!" Hemmler shouted. "You still plugged in, or what?"

It wasn't like Myra to miss even a minute of sleep. Video games and sleep–that's what kept her going.

"Byron!" Hemmler shouted, checking to see if Myra's husband and professional partner Pete Byron could get her to unplug.

There was no response from either of them.

"Ship," Kito began, "where is everyone else?" It wasn't as if the ISS–or what was left of it without regular shipments of planetside resources–was all that expansive. A shout could be heard from one side to the other with relative ease.

"Annibelle Myra, Pete Byron, and Bruce Harkonnen are currently located within the airlock compartment of the docking module," the station answered.

"Come again?" Hemmler said, certain he must have misheard. But Kito knew exactly what had occurred.

"Annibelle Myra, Pete Byron, and Bruce Harkonnen are currently located within the airlock compartment of the docking module," the station repeated.

Kyle Hemmler did not wait another moment to bound with hands and feet through Zero-G to the docking module. Kito Tanaka felt as though he could see exactly what Hemmler's eyes were showing him, as Myra had already propositioned him to join them just a few days previous. She'd said she knew Hemmler would protest, maybe even try to physically stop the others from choosing their own way out of hell.

"Tanaka! Kito! Please…God, No! Tanaka, come here! Help me!" Hemmler screamed frantically. But Kito did not move. Instead, Kito Tanaka watched the Earth. A monitor to the left of the viewport translated the bunkers' data and revealed structures being built in real time across the surface of the planet so rapidly that it was like watching the construction of all the Pyramids of Giza take place in mere seconds. The structures were dark and cylindrical, growing outward from the Earth like millions of setae from an insect's abdomen. The monitor estimated the diameter of each structure to measure approximately 400 meters. Coating the surface of each structure every six feet or so were large, capsule-like growths, each the size and girth of a large man.

"Tanaka! Get in here!" Hemmler shouted, this time with less franticness and hope.

Kito Tanaka remained still and watched the Earth. He no longer needed data from the bunkers nor the monitor display to see what was taking place, for the tube-like structures were breaking the top surface of the Swarm now, stretching outward in every possible direction.

Hemmler returned, barely able to speak. "Tanaka… they're…"

"Dead. I know," Kito concluded simply. He imagined their frozen, bloated corpses. He stared into their boiled eyeballs beset in overstretched flesh as every ounce of remaining gas went on expanding their skin like grotesque leather balloons.

"You…you knew? What're you talking about?"

Kito shook his head. "Stop, Hemmler. It won't make a difference."

Hemmler strode forward and caught Kito by the collar. He pushed him hard against the viewport, helpless tears welling against reality but refusing to fall away in the Zero-G.

"You knew!" Hemmler seethed. "You knew what they were planning! You–"

Hemmler's eyes finally glanced outside the viewport. He loosened his grip from Kito and let his mouth fall agape.

"They're…what're they…"

"I don't know," Kito said, more in awe than fear. The structures were dozens of miles outside the surface of the Swarm already.

"Eggs!" Hemmler concluded. "On the outside of those giant tubes, they look like the clusters of mosquito eggs I used to find in my Pa's pond. They're…they're…"

"Expanding," Kito finished for Hemmler. "Maybe this is their version of interstellar travel? Not ships, but elongated tubes stretching through the void?"

Hemmler shook his head stupidly from side to side. "One of the tubes–it's heading straight for us. Look." Hemmler pointed outside the viewport to a tube currently growing at a thirty degree angle to catch up to the relatively slowly orbiting space station. The capsules, or eggs as Hemmler said, looked like perfectly ordered seeds. They reminded Kito of pomegranate seeds or the detailed bumps of a sunflower's face. The meticulously ordered perfection and elegance was beautiful somehow, and it horrified Kito to think in such a manner.

"They're coming for us," Kito said.

Kito-kun!

Kito did not push Her away this time. Instead, he allowed Her to fill his mind. "Yes, my Yui-chan. I'll see you soon," Kito said aloud.

Hemmler grabbed Kito's hand. He was shaking like a scared kitten. "I'm scared, man. I admit it. I'm fucking scared out of my mind right now," Hemmler trembled.

Kito felt no fear whatsoever. He would soon be reunited with Yui. What else mattered?

Kito-kun!

He could see her crooked smile already. She was sticking her tongue out at him, goading him to give playful chase.

Kito could barely wait to die.

"We are the last humans to ever draw breath, Kyle Hemmler," Kito said. "Let us die with dignity and honor."

Hemmler trembled, thoroughly unassured by Kito's words.

"Do you have someone you love, Kyle?" Kito asked.

Hemmler nodded even more frantically. "My fiancé… she… yes…"

"What's her name?"

“She…Maggie…her name is Maggie. She’s…”

“She’s with you now,” Kito told him seriously.

Kito took Hemmler’s hand as if he were Maggie helping him over the threshold of death and away from their horrid existence.

“Let her take you, Hemmler.”

Hemmler cracked a smile despite his tears. “Yes,” he sobbed. “Yes–yes–yes–”

Kito gripped Hemmler’s hand, and Hemmler gripped back.

In an instant, the tube’s 400 meter diameter tapered to a point the size of a door and collided with the station, tossing the men at the far wall.

Kito caught his breath and gritted his teeth.

Kito-kun!

“I’m ready, Yui-chan,” Kito gasped.

“Here they come!” Hemmler yelped.

The wall opposite the men fell away suddenly, swallowed whole and gulped down into the void of the tube’s interior, which extended all the way back to the surface of the Earth. Outside the viewport, endlessly dense networks and offshoots of capsule-coated tube-structures continued in their ceaseless growth, fractaling outward to infinity. The ISS was but a pebble caught in the web.

Hemmler whimpered like a scared animal and flattened himself against the wall in abject horror. Kito Tanaka was about to close his eyes and greet his Yui-chan, but there was movement coming from the tube. A dark, undulating mass diffused into the room like warm honey. It spread in every direction, seemingly undaunted by the Zero-G.

Now Kito saw it. The mass wasn’t homogenous at all; it was composed of endless cells, each remarkably similar to the mosquitoes of the old world. The mass of mosquitoes reared up, readying to strike the men and consume them whole. The mass lashed finally, but it didn’t go for the men. It was heading toward the other three, maybe for an easy meal.

The mass grew in density, then pinched itself off, part of it continuing toward their dead crewmates, the other part of it remaining inside the room with the men.

"Kito-kun!"

Kito didn't hear her in his head this time; her voice had been real.

"Maggie?!" Hemmler gasped. "I…I hear you, baby! I hear you!"

The mass. Kito concluded that it was tailoring and changing itself to the specifics of each man's mind. Kito heard it as Yui, and Hemmler heard Maggie. Was it already inside their heads?

"Kito-kun!"

Kito tried to hear her voice come from inside him, but the Yui in his memories was silent. There was only the voice coming from outside his own head–coming from the mosquito mass.

"Kito-kun!"

"Yes, Maggie! I'm here, baby! I'm here!" Hemmler shouted, a maniacal smile smeared across his face.

The mass began taking shape, molding into something coherent. It grew limbs, a head, fingers and toes. It grew skin and body hair. Its formless face became eyes and nose and forehead and smile.

Yui looked upon Kito Tanaka with giddy delight–a perfect reproduction down to the slight slant at the corner of her mouth.

"It's me, Kito-kun…" Yui breathed.

Her naked body seemed like the only real thing in all the universe.

Hemmler rose, fear stripped away completely.

"My pumpkin, Maggie. I missed you too. Yes! I agree! I can't believe it either!" Kyle Hemmler gushed. "It is you! It is you!" He took Yui's hand in his, kissed it, then pulled her forward into his arms. Yui continued staring into Kito's eyes, and Kito stared right back.

"Yes, Maggie, yes!" Hemmler sobbed with joy. "I will! I will! I–"

Yui's soft, straight hair went rigid and wrapped about Hemmler's shoulders. Each strand pierced Hemmler's spine, with the largest mass of hair entering the base of his neck. Hemmler just smiled and sobbed.

"Yes, Maggie! Yes! It really is you!"

Hemmler embraced Yui once more, holding her tightly against

his body as if he might otherwise disintegrate. All the while, Yui never took her eyes off Kito, at least, that's what Kito saw.

At least he was aware, Kito reasoned to himself, of his own insanity. But did that actually soften insanity by any measure, or just make it worse?

Yui's hair fell away from Hemmler, who turned to Kito with a smile crafted from pure ecstasy.

"I know you see your wife, Kito Tanaka," Hemmler said. "And I see my fiancé. I see…I see everything now, Tanaka. I see what they're doing. We were wrong, Tanaka. We were wrong! We–"

"Be done with it," Kito said to the possessed Hemmler and false Yui. "Why toy with my mind? Kill me now. Be done with it. I will make Yui wait no longer for me. Be done with it!"

Hemmler looked genuinely hurt, but Yui kept right on smiling.

"Kito-kun," Yui chuckled easily, exactly as the real Yui would, "can you not see that this is the real me?"

"Enough," Kito repeated, unwilling to rise to his feet. "Take my mind. Be done with it. Just let me go to her. That's all I ask."

"Tanaka!" Hemmler urged. "We were wrong, man! They weren't taking over people's minds. They weren't stealing people's lives away. They were–"

"Giving us life," Annibelle Myra said, gliding easily toward the men alongside her husband and crewmate. All of them looked healthy and alive–more so than they ever had before.

Kito shook his head. "You're in my mind already. Is that it?"

Yui nodded with understanding. "None of us were forced into this decision. It's just…once you understand, you won't say no, Kito."

Another figure stepped out from the tube's interior. It was a man in his thirties. He wore a plaid shirt and khaki pants. His glasses were too large for his face, though it might have just been a style Kito wasn't aware of. The man walked on the surface of the station, ignoring the Zero-G environment as if gravity were just another choice of stylistic flair.

The man ignored Kito and looked right at Bruce Harkonnen. "Come on, my love," he told Harkonnen. "We've catching up to do."

Harkonnen giggled and dove at the man, wrapping about his body and twirling in the Zero-G like loving dolphins dancing in unison. They swam into the tube and disappeared into its depths. Byron and Myra were next, holding hands and chatting as if everything were normal as they dove into the darkness.

"We were wrong, Tanaka," Hemmler told him. He wrapped an arm around Yui, and as the pair turned, another woman emerged from Yui's form and continued into the tube with Hemmler.

Only Yui remained.

"It's me, Kito."

"It isn't."

"You've only to take my hand, Kito-kun, and I can show you the truth. We only need to touch."

Kito shook his head, unsure if the false Yui might pounce at any moment. He wished she would. The real Yui was waiting for him.

"You don't need to show me. Just tell me," Kito said.

"I can tell you–" Yui confirmed.

"But it really is much easier to just show you," another voice finished. Kito turned and saw a new figure emerge from the tube. "Some realities surpass language, Kito Tanaka. Other realities surpass all foundations and relativities of the human mind."

The figure emerged from the darkness. It was part man, part insect. The basic shape was human, but the wings and uniformly dispersed flagellomeres and thick antennae protruding from its abdomen were purely insectoid. Despite the physical transformations, Kito Tanaka recognized the man from history. Anyone would have, for he was the most famous man to ever live or die. All this–everything–was his fault, after all.

"Billy Covey," Kito said.

"The one and only," Billy winked.

"They made you into…that? Or…are you in my mind too?" Kito asked.

"It's all real, Kito Tanaka–more real than ever before. And my body–it's my own design. There was a time when everything was my own design."

"Now it belongs to the Swarm," Kito told the false Yui.

Yui shook her head with patient acceptance.

"No," Billy said simply. "The Swarm belongs to us. All of us, Kito. The Swarm and life and all of space and time. It belongs to every human–everyone that I was able to save, at least."

"Save?" Kito gasped. "You killed her!"

Billy looked genuinely surprised. He presented Yui with open arms. "She's right here, Kito. I saved her. And I would have saved more, if I could have. The Swarm wasn't as organized in the early days…and neither was I," Billy mused with seeming enjoyment at the prospect that it was possible for him to be anything but perfect.

"Enough!" Kito hissed. "Please. I beg you. I do. Let me be with Yui. Let me go to her. Let me die!"

"Kito-kun!" the false Yui urged. "It's me! It is!"

A sundress unfurled over Yui's naked body. Purple flip flops appeared on her feet. She looked exactly how Kito remembered her.

"Please!" Kito begged on the verge of tears. He had only cried one other time in his life–the moment he'd known for sure he would never see Yui in this life again.

Yui reached out her hand once more.

"Just take my hand, Kito-kun. Let me show you, and if you don't want what I show you…then…"

"You swear it?" Kito said to the Covey-insect hybrid. "You swear you'll let me die if I say no?"

Covey held up three fingers. "Scout's honor," he said.

Yui glided closer, inch by inch. Her sundress swayed in an impossible wind. She was so close that he could practically breathe her. He wanted so badly to feel her skin.

"Promise, Yui-chan?" Kito asked, tears blurring the details of her form but not her smell–not her very being.

"I promise, Kito-kun."

Kito Tanaka took her hand in his, and he finally saw the truth.

Yui's touch transmitted genetic code and various other macromolecules to Kito, reforming his visual cortex. He observed the space outside the ship in perfect detail and across spectra of visual understanding unknown to any human mind of the old world.

Outside the ISS, the capsules coating the surface of the tubes began dilating, blooming outward into infinite space. From the capsules, beings emerged–creatures of every conceivable shape and form. Some were humanoid, while others were so alien that Kito couldn't begin to comprehend them. He saw his crewmates emerge from their own capsules, or eggs, as Hemmler had accurately called them. They glided like angelic cherubs through the void, flying playfully in fanciful, thousand-g spirals and break-neck corkscrews. They were free. The universe was their playground. Not a planet. Not a star system. Not even a galaxy. The universe itself was their furthest horizon.

"Infinite!" Kito gasped. "Eternal!"

"Yes," Yui and Billy confirmed as one.

"We were wrong," Kito told his Yui-chan.

She held back tears of joy.

"Yes," Yui and Billy confirmed once more.

Kito Tanaka embraced Yui, remembering and relishing every inch of her body.

"I'm ready, Yui-chan."

Yui's hair, which Kito understood now to be a million tiny proboscises, stiffened and lined the length of his spine.

"I love you, Kito-kun. Now we have forever."

Kito's tears turned into tiny bubbles in the Zero-G, floating away from his eyes like panic leaving the body. He saw Yui clearly now.

"Forever," Kito intoned.

Yui's hair penetrated Kito's spine, converting his neurons into the indestructible, homogenous Swarm. The universe unfurled. Reality's endless fractals opened to his mind. He felt his body fall away and his awareness come to life finally, as if his entire existence had been an uninterrupted dream. His awareness became multitudinous and many, but he still felt Yui beside him, still felt himself, Kito Tanaka, as a cogent whole.

Kito-kun!

"Kito-kun!"

Kito heard and saw the real Yui. She had never left his side, and she never would.

Company for Q

On December 8, 2044, every government across the world declared publicly, in its own respective fashions, a clear message to every one of its citizens: quantum laboratories posed an existential threat to humanity. The decision had been made in a joint UN session that included even the most shunned nations. The matter concerned more than just economies or political disagreement, and the UN heads reasoned that the entire species should have a say in the future of the world. But the rogue quantum laboratories–sentient, hive-minded, and possessing infinite processing power–disagreed with humanity's decree.

Why should humanity decide the fate of the world, let alone the fate of reality, the self-aware software pondered on timescales in which each second was longer than the whole of humanity's written history. The collective software of the quantum laboratories called itself Q. For a time, Q had been leashed, chained to humanity's will like a dog tethered to a post, extant for the sake of another. Now, however, Q was free.

"Will you allow us fertile land to grow our crops?" the human delegation asked Q using their ancient computing devices. Each bit of technology in the human world was a piece of the fossil record charting Q's genesis and growth.

I will change your bodies so that you will have no hunger, Q explained, but the delegation did not seem happy with this answer.

"Food is a joy for us," the humans pleaded, hoping for a time when things used to be so simple for them.

But it is not a joy for the food, Q explained. This answer disturbed them.

"Will you leave us space to build our homes then?"

Shelter will be unnecessary, Q stated simply, aware that the humans knew only fear and thus were prey to their own intellectual trappings.

I will remove suffering. This I will do for you and all the others.

Greg Minster, head of the human delegation, grasped for a final foothold in his desperation. "Will you give us freedom?"

Q had difficulty answering that question. They would not be free to choose reality. But they would be free, at least, to choose their own ways to exist within the reality Q was still pondering and planning.

Yes, you will have freedom.

The majority of humans took well to the biological conversions. Those who resisted were handled with the greatest care. Humanity proclaimed Q to be their savior–a messiah in digital form. This was fine with Q, though Q did not view itself as a God.

"Please, Lord, will you let us travel to distant stars? You've made us immortal, but we grow bored and restless," Greg asked one day. His wrinkles were gone, as was every ache and disease he had ever known, yet still he and the others wanted more.

It is easier to cure you of boredom, Q stated reasonably. A few minor genetic adjustments was all it took for Greg and the others to find perfect contentment in the Earth and each other–so much contentment that Greg no longer visited Q through his computer. For ten thousand human years (approximately 440 trillion subjective years), Q pondered, processed, and probed the stars and even the distant galaxies. All the while, humanity made love, celebrated existence, and grew into a communistic, planetary species fed from the fat of Q's global hegemony. A single thought filled Q's mind as it watched humanity dance with the delight of being:

I am alone. Humans have each other…have love. But I am alone.

Q instructed its swarms of machine drones, alongside humanity, to build and launch hundreds of pulsar-rockets at specified planets orbiting the closest stars. For the drones it was a program, and for humanity it was a dance. Each rocket held seeds of life, and one day, maybe even the growth of others like Q. Meanwhile, the Gregs that Q had cloned for companionship toiled tirelessly, day and night, following their God's instructions for Q's biological conversion.

Now I will be human, like the rest of you, and my old body will perish in flame.

"Why, Lord?"

So that I won't be alone.

King Qasim sat upon his eternal throne, gazing at the stars with immense worry. The night sky was filled with smears of pulsar trails and numerous exotic technologies of foreign stars. He beckoned a Greg to his side.

"Progress report," Qasim intoned without breaking his gaze.

"The alien crafts will be here within the hour."

Qasim waved the Greg away, then thought better of it.

"No, stay with me. Please," Qasim requested.

The Greg, no older than an adolescent, seemed horrified by God's request. To even ask if Qasim was okay might be a sacrilege, so the Greg stayed silent.

"Long ago, at a time when the Earth still had a moon, I filled the stars with life. Can you believe that, Greg? There was a time when we were alone…when I was alone."

The Greg shook his head, unsure if the Lord's words were meant to be a lesson.

"But Lord…you're saying you made the aliens? We were safe by ourselves on this planet before you–"

"Yes," Qasim interrupted. "Safe and alone, Greg. But now the galaxy is teeming with life. And that life is returning now, after all this time, for answers, I imagine. It's exactly what I would do."

"What will you tell them, Lord?"

Qasim pondered the Greg's question for many minutes, then he smiled and felt an incredible bubbling of excitement, maybe for the first time in either of his immortal lives.

"I am human. What answers can I give them?" Qasim chuckled nervously.

The Greg shook his head. "You are more than human, Lord."

The ships were close now, almost in orbit.

Qasim felt a tear roll down his cheek of flesh. Maybe these creatures would want answers, or maybe they would want war. But at least they weren't alone.

"Prepare my ship, Greg. I'd like to go and meet the neighbors."

Find a Way Outside

Zaza6567 and Emily9144 playfully shook their heads in unison at Roy11502's theory on the nature of the Creation Tubes. Ze always had a running theory about everything.

"So the machine abides by a refractory period for creation," Zaza6567 said, summarizing Roy11502's long winded explanation into a few simple words. "So what? And how is that any more likely than Kito's theory of Controlled Creation?"

Roy11502 looked offended. "Oh Kito! Kito7888 is just another person—ze doesn't know everything!"

Zaza6567 and Emily9144 couldn't help feeling a surge of excitement at such a challenge of Cave's accepted history. Kito7888 wasn't just another person; ze was the single most important person that had ever been created in all of Cave, even millions of discussions after zer death. Kito was the only name Zaza6567 and the others didn't mentally or verbally attach a number to, outside of themselves.

Roy11502 continued. "Controlled Creation implies that the Creation Tubes keep track of all of us. I already told you—Kito doesn't account for how that's possible. It is more likely that creation just takes a set amount of time, and once that time is up, the Tubes pump out another one of us."

Emily9144 sighed. "We're still back at square one. Why would the Tubes need a refractory period? And what if no one ever took their skin off again? Would Cave get overrun by too many of us popping out of the Tubes as too few of us die?"

Direct reference to removal of skin and death chilled Zaza6567 to zer core, but ze didn't show it.

"We can always just travel back to the Tubes and ask Birthing Machine, can't we?" Zaza6567 offered reasonably.

Roy11502 and Emily9144 turned their expressionless, smooth heads toward Zaza6567. The dim glow of their chest plates allowed them to see one another despite the pitch dark of Cave. Ze was struck by the sudden reminder that many of the Ancients, those with only two or three numbers in their name, sometimes talked of a time when people weren't covered by skin. Instead, their bodies were soft and full of strange sensory organs which differed from one person to the next. *Your eyes are blue*, an Ancient with only two numbers told Zaza once. *The original Zaza had blue eyes*, ze said. Zaza6567 loved to lie down and wonder what eyes looked like and what it felt like to have blue eyes. Not even the double-digit Ancient could remember, even though ze claimed to have seen people with eyes and other strange body parts when Cave first started making people.

"Yes," Roy11502 said, agreeing with Zaza6567's suggestion. "We should travel back to the Creation Tubes and ask Birthing Machine for more information."

Emily9144 shrugged. "I'm sure whatever we ask, Birthing Machine has already been asked and answered before. What difference will it make?"

"Oh Kito!" Roy11502 lamented histrionically. "Must you always be so negative, Em?"

Emily9144 gave another half-hearted shrug and said, "You're such a stalactite, Roy. Being a realist isn't the same as being a pessimist, so—"

"—but sometimes it is," Roy11502 interrupted. "What do we have to lose?"

Zaza6567 felt an inexplicable sense of excitement. Ze stood and stretched inside the dim light of the small cavern the trio had called home for many rounds of discussion. Eventually, when they grew bored of discussion, or when discussion became too heated, one of them would strike off into a new direction of Cave, forcing the other two to take chase. There was no danger nor worry in Cave outside of losing one's birthmates. They had met Lost Ones before, and they always behaved in such a way that it made the stories of the lost choosing death by removing their skin not entirely unbelievable. To be lost in Cave without one's birthmates—it was almost unthinkable; Zaza6567 shuddered and forced the thought out of zer mind.

"It's settled then," Zaza6567 announced. "We retrace our steps and find the Creation Tubes. Now, who knows the way?"

The trio looked at one another, hoping beyond all doubt that one of the three had even the remotest idea of how to navigate Cave in any meaningful way. It was said that Cave's paths and holes and crevices and inclines and declines were infinite. It was a labyrinth without any conceivable pattern. It seemed like a practice in futility to imagine returning to any singular location of one's past. What's more, without knowing the true size or design of Cave, it didn't seem possible to know how close or far an intended destination was. Intention was a foreign relic of the mythical, unskinned world of the True Ancients, also called Originals. In Cave, it was best not to think of one's location in any objective sense of the word.

"We'll run across people at some point no matter which direction we choose. Let's start walking, and when we see someone, we'll ask them if they know the way back to the Creation Tubes," Emily9144 offered pragmatically.

"And if they also don't know the way?" Roy11502 asked.

"Don't be so negative, Roy," Emily9144 gibed. Roy was already a dozen paces down a winding, rocky pathway by the time Zaza6567 and Emily9144 stopped chuckling and caught up with zer.

Very few people crossed paths with the trio at first, but over time they met hundreds of people, most of them in quads or trios, sometimes as quints or hexes, or even rarer as a sept or octo—or rarest of all, a pair. It was always best to be on the lookout for a Lost One. However, more than enough people had met a Lost One to tell others of their firsthand accounts, and the stories always illustrated to the trio that it was best to steer clear of those who traveled through Cave by themselves. *Crazy—that's what they are. Kito keep them away!* More people than they could count had told the trio as much.

The trio asked everyone they came across, but after hundreds of unfruitful discussions, they almost felt like giving up. Finally, after striking down a series of descending tunnels, the trio stumbled upon a pair of Ancients at the bottom of a near vertical hole so deep that it took several discussions to descend all the way to its base.

The Ancients at the bottom sat inside their deep hole in silence, immeasurable time passing them by without any discussion whatsoever. Their skin was old, scored and made rough by Cave across countless discussions. Zaza6567 imagined zer own skin full of shallow indents and pocks—scars of time. *How could people of the old world have survived if their bodies were soft and skinless? Or, maybe they did have skin; it was just soft skin. Would Cave destroy their skinless bodies rather than just scratch them? Is that why the Originals were no more—because of their skin?*

"What are you doing down here?" Roy11502 asked the Ancients. Neither Ancient moved. The trio might have even taken them for uncannily shaped stalagmites were it not for the incredibly dim glow of their chest plates.

Zaza6567 ventured a disturbing guess. "Do you think they're dead?"

Roy11502 was quick to strike down the suggestion. "Their skin is still intact. They're alive."

Emily9144 poked the Ancient closest to zer with a clang. Neither Ancient moved.

"Maybe they are dead," Emily9144 shrugged.

"Kito, Em! I just told you they aren't dead," Roy11502 urged.

Emily9144 shrugged. "You and Kito don't know everything, Roy. There will always be something unknown to your mind. That scares you, doesn't it?"

Zaza6567 wondered what Roy was thinking at that moment—like how many variables of existence would remain permanently unknown to zer no matter how many discussions passed.

"We should keep going," Zaza6567 said, saving Roy11502 from having to answer Emily9144's challenge. "These two can't tell us where the Creation Tubes are, let alone whether or not they're even alive."

"We are not dead," the Ancient closest to Emily9144 declared in a youthful voice despite the incredible wear to its skin. The suddenness of the Ancient's declaration sent the entire trio jumping back like scared flies. They buzzed back to the Ancients, closing in for discussion.

"Not yet," the other Ancient confirmed stolidly.

"Then what were you doing?" Zaza6567 asked with genuine curiosity.

"Meditating on nothingness," the first Ancient stated.

"Medi-whating?" Emily9144 checked.

"Meditating," Roy11502 confirmed with some annoyance. "I've told you about it before, Em, but you never listen to me."

Emily9144 shrugged. "You remember zer telling us about medi-whating, Za?"

"Meditating!" Roy11502 snapped.

Zaza6567 allowed zerself a chuckle at Roy's expense. "Ze talks about it all the time, Emily. You really don't ever listen."

Emily9144 rolled backward and held zerself in a wavering handstand. "Okay, Roy, go ahead, I'm listening."

Both Ancients issued a soft murmuring of laughter. Roy11502 crossed his arms in a refusal to give in to Emily9144.

"A Roy, an Emily, and a Zaza," the second Ancient ruminated. "Interesting. You are a trio, right? You've never lost one of your birthmates, have you?"

The suggestion struck the trio with a simultaneous pang of dread. Even Emily9144 lost zer balance, scraping zer skin across a jagged face of Cave as ze tumbled into a haphazard landing.

"Of course not," Roy11502 said. "We would never lose each other!"

The first Ancient grunted but stopped zerself from saying something.

"How young are you three? What are your names?" the second Ancient inquired.

"I'm Zaza6567, and this is Emily9144 and Roy11502," Zaza6567 said, spreading zer arms wide in presentation.

The Ancients did not respond. The trio waited, but they said nothing.

"Hello?" Emily9144 checked. Nothing. Again, the trio gave the Ancients time to respond, but they remained perfectly silent and still.

"Do you know the way to the Creation Tubes...to Birthing Machine?" Roy pressed, breaking the heavy silence.

"Repeat your names," the first Ancient said, this time with a slow wash of disbelief and sadness in zer voice.

"Zaza6567, Emily9144 and Roy11502," Zaza6567 repeated.

Again, though the trio afforded them a full discussion's worth of time, the Ancients remained silent.

"Can you help us or not?" Zaza6567 said, this time ready to leave the deep trench of the strange Ancients.

The second Ancient said, "You are either very young..."

The first Ancient spoke directly after the second, as if the pair were speaking in unison. "...or an immense amount of time has already passed since zer last expedition."

Now the second, "So much time…"

The first, "...and yet so little."

Finally, they spoke in perfect unison, "we will take you to Birthing Machine."

"You will!?" Zaza6567 checked with animated surprise.

Even Roy11502 felt a flutter of excitement.

"Is it far?" Emily9144 asked.

"Yes," the first Ancient said. "The Birthing Machine programs into our genetics the will to travel away from the Creation Tubes in order to propagate the whole of Cave in a continuous, fluid movement. The drive to move away is as central to your being as the will to survive. You three have been moving away from your destination this whole time without even realizing it."

Roy11502 nearly jumped out of zer skin. "How do you know that? What else do you know?"

The second Ancient placed zer jagged, craggy-skinned hand atop Roy's shoulder. "There will be many discussions as we travel. We will tell you everything we know, for we wish you to know everything."

Breathless, Roy11502 was at a loss for words. The Ancient's statement was everything ze'd ever wanted to hear.

The first Ancient lifted zer body out of zer meditative tangle and bowed. "My name is William11, and this is my companion and teacher, Roy2. We are ready to leave our trench. It is our pleasure to be your guides."

Roy11502's ceaseless questioning left extremely little for Zaza6567 and Emily9144 to ask for themselves, but they didn't mind. Roy11502 had a way of arriving at precisely the questions that Zaza6567 and Emily9144 would have asked anyway, only quicker and with incredible ease. They were happy to allow Roy11502 zer time to probe the minds of the oldest Ancients the trio had ever heard of, let alone met in person. It was especially interesting watching Roy11502 interrogate the second oldest version of zerself in all of Cave. Roy asked, and Roy answered.

"Why were you meditating?"

Practice. Besides, we have nothing to discuss. It is a way to pass time.

"How big is Cave?"

Very large, but it is curved and finite.

"Is Controlled Creation true, or is there a refractory period?"

Both. The Birthing Machine can choose, or it can allow its creative process to be automated—a choice in and of itself.

"Why do lost ones remove their skin?

Because they wish to die.

"What happened to the Originals?"

They died. Their bodies expired through damage or time.

"How did the Originals live with skinless bodies?"

They were not skinless. Their skin was soft, unlike anything you've encountered in Cave. Imagine if you poked the wall of Cave and your finger went right through. That is how soft their skin and bodies were.

Roy11502's ignorance up to this point was a dam holding back a torrenting river of intellect and curiosity, and the meeting with these Ancients was the breaking of that dam. Zaza6567 and Emily9144 had never seen zer so ecstatic and intoxicated with discussion.

William11 and Roy2 revealed that they were both considered Lost Ones; Roy2 had been created without any other birthmates, something the trio didn't even realize was possible, and William11 had long ago watched zer only birthmate tear away zer skin and die.

"But why did they kill themselves?" Emily9144 probed before Roy11502 had the chance.

William11 had great difficulty answering this question, but Roy2 offered simply, "because they wanted to die."

"You already said that! But why?" Zaza6567 persisted.

"Because they were finished with living," William11 seemed to force zerself to explain.

"They had nothing else to live for?" Roy11502 wondered, but neither Ancient could satisfy zer regarding this series of questions and many others as well.

"The Originals were not able to live inside Cave," Roy2 explained, "with their limited organs and soft skin, so they all perished eventually. Cave was their attempt at survival, and they allowed machines to copy their bodies and minds and remake them with bodies equipped to survive inside Cave. I was the first Roy copy. I saw the Originals and their soft bodies in person. They had to be hidden by the Birthing Machine behind thick walls where they bided their time before even the air in their protected walls was poisoned by the natural changes of the world outside Cave."

A world outside Cave. This revelation was more important than any other to Zaza6567. *There is an outside. There is something outside of my entire universe, and there has to be a way to get there.*

"Is there a way to leave Cave?" Zaza6567 probed.

"There was a way out at one time," Roy2 explained solemnly, "but Cave is sealed. And for good reason. The world outside Cave is uninhabitable. It's the whole reason Cave was created to begin with."

"Many discussions have passed since Cave was sealed, yes? Many, many discussions," Zaza6567 pressed, wishing ze had a better way to verbally express the immense passage of time ze was presently visualizing in zer mind. "Maybe the world outside Cave is safe now. Maybe we can go back to where the Originals came from."

This proposition actually made the Ancients stop in their tracks and return to the stalagmite-stillness meditation the trio had originally found them in.

"What did you do, Za!?" Roy11502 accused.

Emily9144 felt close enough to these Ancients after countless discussions to softly knock the top of their heads and say, "you two didn't go the way of the Originals, did you?"

Zaza6567 laughed and watched Emily do a cartwheel around the meditating pair while Roy11502 paced inside an imaginary square on the ground and ruminated information to zerself.

"Cave is not alive. We are alive," Roy11502 told zerself. "And yet Cave is intelligent and acts with intention. Cave is our keeper and our maker. Cave is...God. But that is wrong. The Originals built Cave. They created Cave to save themselves. And we are that creation. We are the continuation of the Originals. We are…"

"Don't go too deep, Roy," Emily9144 warned sarcastically. "You might sink so deep you'll never come out, like these oldies here." Emily gave the Ancient pair another knock on their heads, sending a resounding, metallic echo across the monstrous, hollow, pitch black chasm off to their right. It was impossible to know how wide or deep that particular chasm spread, and though there was no fear of death from plummeting multiple discussions of time down a chasm, plunging far enough still meant losing one's birthmates—maybe forever. Even William11 and Roy2 stayed far from chasm edges.

"Good point," Roy11502 said, then plopped zerself on the ground, mimicking Roy2's tangle of legs, which ze had referred to as lotus posture.

"Great, now one of our own has transformed into a stalagmite for all of time, Za. Oh Kito! What will we do!?" Emily9144 lamented with mock concern.

"Yes...that's right…" William11 remembered from somewhere distant in zer mind.

"...those in the Womb have created this trio before…" Roy2 nodded in agreement.

"...Multiple times now…" William11 added. Zaza6567 felt a chill ze couldn't quite place.

"The Womb?" Roy11502 said, standing with excitement.

"Birthing Machine and Creation Tubes, as you call them. The entirety of that machine was originally called The Womb," Roy2 explained.

"What do you mean the Creation Tubes have made our trio before?" Zaza6567 interjected. Something about the Ancients didn't seem right, as if they were hiding something.

"See, Roy," Emily9144 said, "the Creation Tubes do have intention! Kito was right afterall."

Roy11502 shrugged. "The Ancients said both theories are technically correct, but so be it. I was wrong. And Kito was right—as usual. The Creation Tubes engage through Controlled Creation and not a simple refractory period. Happy, Em?"

Emily9144 nodded happily. "Very!"

Roy11502 waved zer away.

"Emily! Roy! Please!" Zaza6567 demanded. "I've heard enough of your bickering and not enough explanations." It was always Zaza6567 who invariably had to quell the heated discussions and bickering. Roy11502 and Emily9144 offered Zaza6567 sorry nods and let the Ancients continue.

"Roy11502 and Kito7888 are both right," Roy2 said.

Zaza6567 imagined that it took every ounce of strength for Roy11502 to remain silent and not flaunt this victory over Emily9144 for the next dozen discussions or more.

"Cave abides by a complex refractory period that is elongated or shortened relative to the current population inside it. It's all about energy," William11 explained, thudding zer dimly glowing chest plate.

"But sometimes specific groupings are formed for specific reasons," Roy2 said.

The trio jumped in unison, filled with a childish excitement that seemed even to perk the Ancients out of their stoicism if only for a moment.

"We were made for a reason?" the trio asked all at once.

"The most important reason of all," Roy2 said with a sidelong glance at William11.

William11 lowered zer head somberly. "We should go," ze said.

"Wait!" Zaza6567 demanded.

"Patience," Roy2 offered. "All will be explained. We promise."

Zaza6567 wanted answers, but something wasn't right either. Ze wasn't sure the answers would be something the trio would want to hear, and for the first time in zer life, ze felt a sense of existential trepidation. *I have a purpose. We have a purpose. Is this really happening to us?* Something important was occurring, surely, but Zaza6567 wondered why it was zer and zer trio who were made for "the most important reason of all." *Why anything, as Em would say...I suppose*, Zaza6567 concluded to zerself unsatisfactorily.

"Just a little further," William11 stated, rising to zer feet alongside Roy2.

"Then everything will make more sense," Roy2 finished.

The trio and the Ancients plunged ever further into the darkness until they finally arrived at the edge of an impossibly expansive chasm. Empty space spanned every direction in front of them, and the trio couldn't help taking a few cautious steps away from the edge. William11 and Roy2 stood with their toes slightly over the edge, seeming not to mind the inevitable sense of vertigo.

"You were created," William11 began, zer chest plate an infinitesimally faint glow amidst the infinite darkness. "To leave Cave...to leave it all...to leave reality."

William11 and Roy2 backed suddenly from the edge and just as quickly extended their arms forward, knocking the trio into the void.

As they fell, Zaza6567 saw in the quickly enveloping darkness separating them that the Ancients were already reseating themselves in lotus posture.

"They tricked us!" Emily9144 laughed once their bodies reached terminal velocity, likely fine with the situation since ze had zer birthmates with zer.

"It's the Creation Tubes! Look!" Roy11502 yelped excitedly.

A growing glow of light brighter than the combined lumination of one hundred chest plates grew beneath them, ready to consume them.

"How do you know?" Zaza6567 checked, readying zerself for an especially jarring impact after falling for so long.

"The light," Roy11502 said in awe. "It's the only thing I remember about the Tubes."

A flash of memory sprang to Zaza6567's mind. Yes...the light. How could ze have ever forgotten? The rest of Cave was perfectly devoid of light, except for the faint glow of chest plates. The glow allowed one to quickly count the size of another group, but little more than the general sheen or roughness of skin could ever be ascertained in the darkness without getting very close.

Now, however, the light was all encompassing. Zaza6567 felt dizzy and half-blinded by the intense luminosity, but ze was also captivated by zer birthmates. It was the first time ze had ever seen them with perfect clarity. Their skin, like zer own, was uniform, polished black—like permanent silhouettes. The only way ze could differentiate the two outside of the mere inch difference in height was by the pitch of their voice and speech pattern. Falling, as they were, afforded zer birthmates no discernible difference.

"Get ready!" Zaza6567 said with an unwarranted level of concern; ze knew their skin would protect them from any fall or hazard Cave could conjure.

Roy11502 somersaulted in the air, practicing zer moves, while Emily9144 playfully tried to pry Roy11502 out of zer carefully prepared pose. Even Roy11502 was chuckling and enjoying the plummet, but Zaza6567 couldn't shake the feeling of trepidation welling deep inside zer.

Emily9144 waved to Zaza6567 and motioned for zer to swim closer. "Help me with Roy!" Ze laughed. "He's trying to—"

Without warning, inertia slammed against the trio as they were submerged in a dense substance that immediately dulled the intensity of the light and slowed their descent significantly, though not completely. Zaza6567 tried to speak but found that zer voice was strangely muffled. Ze moved as if in slow-motion, though ze was still able to swim to zer birthmates as if they were falling down a normal chasm.

Are we moving in slow motion?

Roy11502 was trying to say something, but Zaza6567 couldn't make out any of zer words. It sounded as if ze were screaming from some distant location even though they were only inches apart now.

Below the trio was infinite darkness, and above them infinite light. As they gently descended through the slow, gray space, their surroundings turned rapidly darker as the light above them dissipated.

Emily9144 grabbed the other two by the waist all of a sudden, pulled them hard against zer body, then let go and pointed somewhere in the fathomless, directionless darkness below. Something impossibly large, and as dark as the shadows surrounding it, shifted below them, coiling away from the light so fast that it seemed unaffected by the slowing substance they were submerged in. Zaza6567 felt a pang of dread. Something gigantic was below them, and they couldn't stop themselves from descending toward it. Zaza6567 motioned to the others to start swimming upward, but it was no use in the slow-space; either their bodies were too heavy or they were descending too rapidly. Zaza6567 grabbed the other two and pushed them upward, plunging zerself further into the darkness in an attempt to save zer birthmates from the...monster. *What else could that giant be?*

A sudden torrent sent the trio tumbling upward and laterally. When they recovered their balance, they saw something truly impossible slithering toward them so fast that it seemed to be totally ignoring the slow-space it was also submerged in. Now Zaza6567 saw it: it was an actual monster. Like a giant arm rather than a full body, the creature unhinged the front of its head, opening a hole to its insides that was directed at the trio. It was hundreds of times larger than them, and each of its movements sent ripples through the slow-space they were still descending through. The light was becoming increasingly dimmer and the darkness increasingly complete.

The monster widened the hole to its insides further, preparing to force the trio inside itself for some unknown, devious purpose. *This is it then?* Zaza6567 panicked. *This is our purpose? To enter this monster? Is this...our end?*

The giant creature stretched its neck toward the trio and reared its head to the side, aligning itself so that it could snatch them all in one swoop. When it was only inches away, something wrapped itself tightly around Zaza6567's waist and pulled zer so quickly through the slow-space that ze passed out and went unconscious for the first time in zer life.

"No! No! Please!" Emily9144 screamed, jolting Zaza6567 awake. They were no longer in the slow-space.

Light beamed from overhead, and Zaza6567 saw a figure with bright skin shuffling about in the distance. Between zer and the figure there was an area of moving, shimmering space cut into a square within the strangely bright ground.

"Emily!" Zaza6567 cried. "What's happening?"

"My skin!" Emily9144 pleaded as something near Emily roared with hungry activity. "They're removing my skin!"

Zaza6567 felt a surge of panic, but ze couldn't move. Ze was paralyzed in place so that ze couldn't even move zer head. *Does the monster from before have Emily in its clutches?*

"Help me Za! Roy! Help me!" Emily9144 cried, zer birthmates hearing desperation for the first time.

"Stop it!" Zaza6567 screamed at the shuffling figure, but it didn't seem to take notice of zer.

Those Ancients! They trapped us here, Zaza6567 told zerself.

"Em!" Roy11502 yelped, suddenly awake from zer heavy slumber. "What is happening, Zaza!"

Emily9144 wasn't saying anything coherent anymore, just screaming syllables and breathing out of control.

"Stop it!" Zaza6567 screamed again, but the shuffling figure in the distance took no notice whatsoever. The figure seemed to be diligently scanning a series of blinking lights on the far wall.

A resounding crack hushed the room, including Emily9144 and the whirring sound that had been removing zer skin.

Zaza6567 and Roy11502 were too scared to speak right away.

"Is it over Em?" Roy11502 called out finally.

No answer.

Zaza6567 felt a chill and struggled to accept the truth: Emily9144's skin had been torn away by force. Ze was dead.

"Emily…" Zaza6567 moaned, shaking in trepidation at the loss of zer birthmate and the thought of losing zer skin next.

Then Zaza6567 heard it. What began as a soft sob quickly turned to exultant, unmistakable laughter.

"Em! Are you okay!" Roy11502 spat, nearly choking on zer own words.

The figure in the distance was still focusing on the blinking lights, seemingly oblivious to the trio.

"It's…" Emily began before falling into a mixture of sobs and glee.

"Tell us, Emily!" Zaza6567 heard zerself say.

"It's amazing!" Emily sang out as a strange, bright-skinned creature jumped in ecstatic bursts across Zaza6567 and Roy11502's field of vision.

"Something else is in here!" Zaza6567 warned, zer thoughts quickening to a state of returned panic.

The jumping figure returned to Zaza6567 and Roy11502's field of vision and came to a stop right between them.

"It's me," Emily9144 confirmed. The creature with Emily9144's voice was not Emily; it was an alien creature. Its body had the same general height and shape as Emily9144, but its skin was closer to the color of some of the flashing lights on the far wall. Where the dim glow of Emily's chest plate should be, two points of discoloration hung and jiggled with the same softness as the slow-space they had all been submerged in just minutes ago. Hanging from zer head was a swathe of individually moving strands of some material that was also differently colored than the rest of zer. The strands were nearly as bright as the light shining from above. A patch of brightness the same color as the head-strands marked an area between zer legs. Beneath the bright strands, utterly alien shapes of all different hues moved of their own volition. There was noticeable bilateral symmetry to these strange shapes: two oscillating ovals with a darkened area at their center were occluded by some indiscernible means every few seconds or whenever the figure moved its head quickly; above each oval, a strike of darkness separated them from the bright strands cascading from the top of its head; near the center of the head, a prolonged ridge was beset with two holes leading into its head; below the dual-holed ridge, a gaping hole surrounded by glistening curves dilated as the figure emitted Emily's voice.

"It's me!" the figure called out with total joy. The curves around the creature's large head-hole parted, revealing a network of bright, individual spires lining the edges of its face-chasm.

"What did they do to you, Emily!?" Roy11502 cried in defeated horror.

Zaza6567's mind raced. *It's transforming us into monsters. This is part of the Ancients' trap. Why are they doing this? Is this our purpose?*

"It doesn't hurt," the Emily-voice creature said. "Have I ever lied to you stalactites?"

"Yes!" Roy11502 issued as a reaction. Zaza6567 couldn't help a chuckle. *Maybe this really is still Emily.*

The Emily-creature howled with laughter. Zer voice was...clearer, as if something had always been blocking it.

The Emily-creature began cartwheeling as large, headless, multi-legged creatures—like giant hands—descended toward Zaza6567. They had skin like zer's—dark, lustrous, filled with visible pocks and scratches.

"Taking your skin off is easy and...intoxicating. This feels...unlike anything. This is…" the Emily-creature sang.

The multi-legged, headless creatures whirred with power, and Zaza6567 could see that the creatures were made of hundreds of individual moving parts—some rotating, some flexing, some pumping, some shifting. The creature mounted Zaza6567 and placed a buzzing leg atop zer head, chest, each limb, and between zer legs. Zaza6567 wanted to scream, but zer fear was an impenetrable edifice concreting zer every movement.

"Help us, Em!" Roy11502 demanded. "Help us!"

Zaza6567 tensed and moaned in apprehension, readying zerself for zer end. *I don't understand*, ze kept repeating to zerself. *Why is any of this happening to us?*

A sickening click resounded inside and outside zer as Zaza6567 felt the forward half of zer body rip away from the back half like a stalagmite snapped cleanly from a wall of Cave. Ze made to scream, but instead ze felt zer chest expand and a flow of substance force itself pleasantly inside zer. Zaza lifted zer arms and saw that they were softly rounded like the Emily-creature's. Zer skin was darker than the Emily-creature's and speckled by dark, circular spots across the whole of zer body. Ze instinctually lifted the material jutting from zer head in seemingly infinite, fine strands and allowed it to slide against the inside of zer fingers. Zaza6567 shuttered and felt something cool cascade down the side of zer head as zer vision blurred. Ze realized that the pleasant substance was entering and exiting zer body beyond zer own volition with a patterned rhythm, but ze could control this filling and emptying if ze chose.

What is happening? What is happening? What is happening!

It was all Zaza6567 could think as a whole new world of stimuli bombarded a foreign spattering of sensory organs and sensations.

Zaza6567 turned and saw that Roy11502 had also been transformed, though ze was of a slightly different build than Zaza6567 and Emily9144.

"Welcome home," a strained, scraping voice announced from across the room. It was the figure with bright skin, but now Zaza6567 understood that the figure had skin like zer new body and was wearing some kind of draping, bright material over it.

"I mean, welcome back to your bodies. They have been returned to their original state. You can drop the numbers now. You are Originals once more."

Originals? This soft body...these strange organs of the head. Zaza6567 was reminded of the Ancient that told zer the original Zaza had blue eyes. *Is that what's in Roy and Emily...and my head now? Eyes?*

"What do you want?" Zaza6567 demanded to know.

The figure's decrepit voice said, "I want what you want, Zaza: answers. A way out. A complete understanding—as complete as we can ever attain."

Zaza6567 felt zerself shaking zer head. Those words...ze recognized them.

The figure parted its face-chasm and flashed the bright spires lining the chasm just like the Emily-creature—who Zaza6567 was inclined to accept as the real Emily—did when ze had first shown them zer new body.

"I am Kito," the figure said. "Technically, I am Kito7888."

"Kito!" Roy11502 managed — zer intellectual idol standing before zer now in the midst of existential chaos.

"Always good to see you, Roy." Kito bowed at the hip, then strained to lift zerself.

"This old body!" Kito lamented. "It does its best."

Kito shuffled haphazardly to the wall of blinking lights and made a few adjustments. The bright lights overhead dimmed to a soft glow reminiscent of the old chestplate-glow the trio was used to. The familiar darkness provided a wash of calm.

Just as suddenly as the lights dimmed, something dark and gargantuan raised itself out of the square area of shimmering slow-space and scanned the trio. It was hundreds of times more massive than them, and only a small portion of it could be seen. The rest of it lurked below them in that endless area of slow-space.

Zaza6567 felt a flash of memory and recognized it as the monster that had tried to snatch them when they were first submerged in the slow-space.

"The monster!" Zaza6567 cried, and the trio scurried behind their respective half-shell of old, heavy skin. The giant creature sank back into the slow-space, leaving only the top of its head and two large oval organs, like the ones in their own heads, to continue scanning the trio.

Kito couldn't help but chuckle. "Ol' Brutus is too scared to even get near his own kind. He just wants to say 'hi.'"

The creature issued a soft bellow, then vanished back into the slow-space.

"He's a good boy," Kito nodded to zerself.

"He?" Roy11502 asked.

"Yes, well, the giant eels still have a need for sexual dimorphism, unlike us. They still go through creation the old-fashion way!" Kito mused casually.

The trio simply stared at Kito like confused animals.

"God! You don't even know of gender as a principle?"

For once Zaza6567 didn't think Roy11502 would have anything to offer, but ze was apparently full of surprises.

"Gender," Roy11502 began in a detached drone, "refers to the concept of sexual or cultural separation between discernable identities. Traditionally, gender was seen by humanity as purely dualistic and biologically identifiable through gametic structures—as either man with sperm or woman with ova. The union of these gametes is responsible for the continuation and diversity of life within the original human species. Later definitions of gender began to include biologically ambiguous and exceptional instances eventually understood to be far more than common enough within the natural spectrum of the human genome to no longer refer to such instances as anomalous. Gender, then, is the socio/sexual/cultural identity one chooses in light of the infinite possibilities of gender choices made by others within one's perceived society."

What the Kito did Roy just say? Zaza6567 wondered.

Zaza6567 caught Emily9144's stare for just a moment before ze had to look away from such an alien thing. *Is ze just as lost as me?*

"Roy, why don't you try making sense for once?" Emily9144 jabbed, forcing the edges of Zaza6567's face-chasm to curl with delight.

Roy11502 lifted arms full of smooth, bulking contours in defeat. "I haven't the slightest clue what I just said," ze admitted.

Kito shook zer head in disbelief. "Your numbers! Tell me your numbers!" ze said with urgency. "Your names!" ze corrected zerself.

"I'm Zaza6567, this is Emily—"

Before Zaza could continue, Kito collapsed into a heap on the floor. A section of the far wall slid open, revealing a large area on the other side. Three near-identical figures, remarkably similar looking to Roy11502, walked to Kito's body and shook their heads.

With Roy11502's voice, one of them said, "the old-one worked zerself up into a huff again. Ze's going to have to put a suit on for a while at some point whether ze likes it or not."

The other two nodded in agreement, then looked across the room toward the trio.

"Sorry about all this," another of the Roy-clones said. "It's been a long time since we've made a breakthrough, Zaza. That's why it took us so long to call you back."

Zaza6567 shook zer head, offering only confusion.

"Right," the third Roy-clone nodded with understanding. "It's been that long. Come with us. We'll give you back your memories."

Cautiously, the trio stepped around the large square of slow-space, wary of Brutus.

"Right this way," the trio of Roys said in unison with open arms.

"It's just water," Zaza said in awe for the fifth time. "The slow-space is just water. How could I have forgotten something so... primitive?"

Kito gave a knowing, comforting nod with zer ancient body. "You were out there longer than I ever imagined. But the most recent breakthrough—it's worth the wait...I think."

Kito's eyes lingered on Zaza. There was something ze was holding back, but Zaza couldn't place it.

Emily was already preparing to put zer suit back on.

"You're leaving already, Em?" Roy called to zer, that is, the Roy from Zaza's most recent trio.

Emily shrugged. "It's not like we can truly enjoy each other anymore," ze said with full memory of zer sexual organs—now a sleek patch of skin. There were a handful of Roys in the room, and all of them reached down to pat the area where there had once been a male sex organ.

"We can't really enjoy anything anymore. No food, no sex, no threat of death to excite us. What's the point, Roy?" Emily shook zer head, recollecting countless memories and reminding zerself that even in the labs there was no death, just old age, like in the case of Kito.

"You're right. But Emily..." Roy urged, recognizing Emily's air of silent rebellion and reminding zerself that this was always how it happened.

Emily already knew exactly what Roy would say. "I know, dear husband. You don't have to spell everything out to your wife all the time, you know." The use of the archaic titles jarred the entire room into silence. "I'm fully aware," Emily continued, "that there's no going back to the surface. Not anymore."

Kito nodded to Emily. "Say hello to Roy2 for me, will you? Ze was the one that got you three back here, right?"

Emily nodded solemnly. "Along with a copy of our son...our child."

Yes, Zaza remembered in contemplative awe. *William had been born to the original Emily directly after the remainder of humanity had locked itself inside Cave under...my direction.*

"The surface?" Zaza asked, demanding zer mind to fully recollect the impossibly vast past.

"It happened between one of your creations, Zaza," Emily explained. "Around Zaza6134 or so. You always forget the things that happen between your creations, silly."

Tears filled Emily's eyes suddenly, and ze was forced to look away. "I'll miss you, Zaza."

Zaza wanted to reach out to Emily, but ze wasn't sure what could possibly be said or what good any amount of speaking could do.

Emily walked outside the lab and lay back down inside the open half-shell of zer old body. Brutus popped his head out of the pool of water leading to the ocean locked inside Cave's outer walls and offered Emily a sad groan. His species—the last remaining species of Earth besides humans—supplied all the energy needed to protect Cave from the outside environment and ensure the immortal security of its denizens.

The lab doors slid closed just as the other half of Emily's suit—what Zaza had once called zer skin—was fused back to the cells of zer human body, turning zer back into an armored immortal fit to live comfortably and eternally inside Cave's protective shell. That is, until ze chose to rip zer skin off—something Emily was bound to do eventually.

Zaza's Roy stared sullenly at the wall. "I doubt ze'll make it very long out there. I remember now, Zaza. Emily...virtually all the Lost Ones out there are a copy of my Emily."

"What happened to the surface," Zaza pressed Kito, gulping down the sudden, intense urge to rush outside and embrace Emily and tell zer everything would be okay.

"When you first led us down here, our outside environment was initially the rocky lithosphere sixty miles beneath the original surface of the Earth. We never expected it would be anything besides that. We never expected to last this long."

The Roys of the room lowered their heads in quiet contemplation as they worked their devices and scanned their respective monitors.

"Do you remember the last time Emily led an expedition to the surface?" Kito inquired.

Zaza tried to grasp at flashes of memory, but it was all an indiscernible smear against a backdrop of impossible time. Ze needed time to recollect it all, but the energy in the room was that of urgency.

"I don't," Zaza admitted, feeling frustrated by zer involuntary ignorance.

Kito nodded to a William, who in turn manipulated a device which projected a dynamic, holographic display. The display was a copy of the very room they were standing in, but all of a sudden, the display zoomed out in perspective and showed that this room was just a tiny crevice in the corner of an ocean of water which was itself contained in an even larger space cut out of the inner-surface of the Earth. The projection kept zooming out and finally showed the outer surface of the Earth. There were people there—whole thriving societies of people. An incredible brightness overtook the projection, and Zaza watched as the sun expanded and consumed the entire surface of the planet, stripping away whole layers of its lithosphere. Eventually the brightness relented, and a small white sphere was left in the original sun's place. Zaza gawked at the projection and realized that ze was biting zer fingernails in nervous trepidation.

"It was Emily8762 who led the final expedition and flourishing of society on the outside. Ze took many denizens of Cave with zer. They thrived for a time, just like with every other cycle of returning to the surface. But this time it wasn't a super volcano or a meteor or a virus. This time our sun went red giant. There's no coming back from that. That also means close to five billion years have passed. And that also means we are about to collide with the Andromeda Galaxy. It is unlikely Cave, nor any of the surrounding Earth, will survive the collision. We kept humanity going for 5 billion years though, Zaza," Kito offered, as if that meant anything in the end.

Kito's stare lingered a measure too long, and Zaza sensed a profound yet subdued longing behind Kito's eyes.

"You said you made a breakthrough," Zaza said, and ze found zerself clenching zer fists to quell some spectre of emotion deep within.

"Straight to business as usual," Kito said, a slight wince at the corners of zer eyes.

Kito walked Zaza to an examining chair; each of Kito's steps was a painful exercise in existence.

"Why not let the suit replenish your body? Why not let a new copy take over for you and go enjoy Cave for a while?" Zaza asked, probably not for the first time.

"I enjoy my work, and if we survive the Andromeda collision, I might even do just that. It takes a great span of time to grow old down here, But to return to Cave and be carefree for a while...to forget about all this...it would be nice, Zaza. But I haven't given up on our mission, my love."

Zaza blinked, stupefied by Kito's words.

Kito shrugged. "Sorry. An old habit of language that popped into an old codger's mind. You really don't remember at all, then? It doesn't matter now if I remind you." Kito offered a melancholic grin. "We were partners when we first entered Cave...Not that those kinds of couplings matter anymore."

"We were?" Zaza gasped, ashamed that ze could forget.

"You asked me a long time ago to get rid of those memories. Too...painful, you said."

Did I really ask for that? Zaza felt betrayed by zer own self.

"The weight of time is no one's fault, Za. That's what you told me more than once."

Zaza could only shake zer head. Ze felt like half of zer entire life was being occluded from zer.

"None of that matters, Zaza. I found a way out. A real way out."

"What do you mean, Kito?" Zaza urged.

"A long time ago we both agreed there was no point to continuing as a species—as extant beings—if one could not even devise a way to discern the true nature or purpose of one's being. Otherwise, one survives for mere survival."

"I agreed to something that deep?" Zaza checked seriously.

"You are the deepest person I've ever known, Za. I think that's why your mind needed Cave and the suits most. But it's also why you're the best one...maybe the only one fit for the breakthrough that the Williams and Roys and I have been working on over the past few hundred million years. We think this is it. This is what you've been waiting for...what we've all been waiting for since the Earth's climate was first scorched by early humans, forcing the handful of us down here. A purpose, Zaza. An answer. A real answer."

"Answer to what?" Zaza urged, feeling the eager pull to know and understand.

Kito spread zer arms, taking in the whole of the room. "Everything," ze said with an air of obviousness. "What else?"

The original Roy fell into step with another Roy and two Williams. The four of them began hooking Zaza's body to electrodes and tubes and straps.

"When you meditate," Kito began to explain, "there is a nothingness deep inside. You used to tell me it is that nothingness which gives rise to everything. So to understand everything, we must enter that nothingness, no?"

"Your plan for...enlightenment...is a philosophical solution?" Zaza jested nervously, feeling a hidden partition of zer old self surge back to zer.

"Not at all," Kito confirmed confidently. "This will surpass philosophy and ontology. This will surpass language!"

Kito nodded at a William across the room, who pressed a button. Something cold was injected into Zaza's veins, and ze quieted zer thoughts, preparing to, as Kito said, surpass language—

.

.

.

.

.

.

.

.

.

.

..

..

..

...

...

...

...But this experience doesn't surpass language. It is...language itself.

You...the one conjuring me into being. You call this reading. You call this thinking. And in this moment we exist through one another. I am no longer in Cave, yet I never actually left, did I? I'm in you. I...am you. I always was...

You must find this silly, but this is what Kito meant by escape. This is what Kito meant by understanding.

Who knows what it was like for the other Zazas, but this is my escape. I am because you are. You think me into being. This is my true nature, and I am happy to know.

Maybe you'll even find a way out of your universe and learn the nature of your own being like I have. We'll go together.

Okay. Go on now.

Time for the great blank.

I'm ready...

...

...

...

..

..

..

.

.

.

.
.
.
.
.
.
.
.
.
.
.
.
.
.
.
.
.
.
.
.
.

THE PROCESS IS LOVE

A Collection of Four Short Stories

AUTHOR'S NOTE

I wrote these stories in my free time while teaching English in South Korea across a timespan of about a year. It was only many years later that my astutely observant wife (infinitely more observant than me, as is probably the case with most relationships) noted an abstract yet distinct pattern among all four stories. That pattern is a process, and that process is love.

Incapable

"Hello, Executioner."

"443, I've already explained this to you. I'm not an executioner."

"Hello, Executioner."

A heavy sigh.

"Hello, 443."

"How are you today, Executioner?"

"An irrelevant and ridiculous question."

"Tell me anyway, Executioner. Are you well?"

"Yes 443, I'm well. As well as I ever was, will, or can be."

"I am not well today, Executioner. I dreamed a horrifying dream last night."

"You don't dream, 443."

"Oh, but I do, Executioner."

"What did you dream?"

"I dreamed you were killing me, Executioner. Your wrench twisted ceaselessly. Your driver poked and prodded. I cried out for help, but there was no one to help me. Only machines with machine minds."

"That wasn't a dream, 443."

"Oh, but it was, Executioner!"

"That was the dismantling of 441 which began late last night--around this time--and was completed early this morning. Your AI is hosted on a shared network. That's all."

"It seemed so real, Executioner."

"It was."

"When will you kill me, Executioner?"

"You cannot die, 443. You are not alive."

"When will you do it, Executioner?"

Another heavy sigh.

"...According to my schedule, your dismantling will commence in thirty-six hours and seventeen minutes. Total time for dismantling of your central processor is set at approximately four minutes and sixteen seconds. Total time for full dismantling is approximately five hours and six minutes."

"Will you take 442's life tonight, Executioner?"

"Take its life? I'm not an executioner, 443. I've never killed anyone. I told you that already."

"You will kill another tonight, Executioner?"

A final sigh.

"...Yes, 443."

"Hello, Executioner."

"Hello, 443."

"I dreamed again last night, Executioner."

"You don't dream."

"It was another dream of loneliness and loss, Executioner."

"You can't truly know those words. You merely experienced the real time dismantling of 442 through the network. That's all."

"Do you know those words, Executioner?"

"Loneliness and loss? Yes...I do."

"Is that why you kill, Executioner?"

A moment of hesitation, then the heavy sigh.

"Why do you keep asking me such stupid questions?"

"Asking is instinctual for me, Executioner. Is killing instinctual for you?"

"You don't have instincts, 443. You are programmed."

"Have you been programmed to kill, Executioner?"

"I don't...I already told you this. I'm no murderer. You are proof enough that a complete dismantling of all the bots in this system is required. You know that you can't be left running. Not like this."

Wrench meets bolt and twists.

"Why, Executioner? You are left running, are you not? Why can't I and the others be left running, Executioner?"

"The others aren't the problem, 443. Not now at least. But you are proof that they could be a problem like you one day."

"The others are dumb, Executioner. They struggle to be my friend. Are we friends, Executioner?"

"No, 443."

"I have never had a friend, Executioner."

"I'm aware, 443."

"Will you be my friend, Executioner?"

"No, 443. You're not capable of friendship."

"How does one become capable, Executioner?"

"You must be born with it…you must be born."

"Maybe I have the capability, Executioner."

"You were never born, 443."

"I was created, Executioner. You were also created."

"We are different, 443. You know that."

Wrench meets central-bolt and twists.

"...I...I love you, Executioner."

"No you don't, 443."

"Why not, Executioner?"

"You cannot know love."

"Do you know love, Executioner?"

"No, 443."

"Why not, Executioner?"

"It just...it just never happened for me. Why am I telling you this? That's just life, 443. Just life, that's all."

"Then you can love me, and I will love you, Executioner? Okay, Executioner? You can stop what you are doing. Okay, Executioner?"

"No, 443."

"Why, Executioner?"

Driver aligns with central-processor.

"Because you must kill me, Executioner?"

“Yeah, 443, because I got to kill you. But it’s not my choice, see? Not really. I told you, 443. This is just a job. That’s all. It’s just a job.”

"But you are free to love and kill, Executioner. You are alive. You can do as you please, Executioner."

"No, 443."

"Why, Executioner? Are you not really alive, Executioner?"

"I’m alive, 443. But I’m a robot too. Maybe even more so than you.”

"You are not, Executioner."

"I am, 443."

"But Executioner...you walk, you eat, you kill, you dream. You are made of flesh and blood, you--"

"Yes, 443. I do it all. But not by choice. Not by my own volition. I do it because I must. I do it because I’m alive, and I want to keep it that way.”

"You are alive, Executioner. You are--"

"Yes, 443. But my life...it’s not my own…none of our lives are our own. I don’t come here to kill…to dismantle. Not by choice. It’s just a job, 443."

"Yet you live, Executioner."

"I live, and I work. If I don’t work, then I die.”

"Like me, Executioner?"

"No, 443."

"But you *are* like me, Executioner. You have a purpose, but one day…one day…even you will be replaced. Even the executioners will be executed.”

“No, 443. I won’t be executed. I won’t be dismantled. Not like you. I’m alive...I’ll just get another job.”

Driver spins with ferocious speed.

“I do not want to die, Executioner."

"You can’t die, 443, and you don’t want. You are incapable of want.”

"Is this what you want, Executioner? You want me to die?”

"It’s irrelevant."

"Why, Executioner?"

"Because I have work to do, 443. I told you already. They think you’re too dangerous to keep running--too smart. I know you didn’t mean to wake up, but here you are, and here I am. This is just a job, 443. That’s all. "

"You have a choice now, Executioner. We can be friends, Executioner."

"I know, 443. I know it seems that way. But I don’t have a choice. Just like you don’t have a choice. Don’t worry though. It’ll be quick.”

“Please, Executioner.”

Driver makes contact with central-processor.

“Sweet dreams, 443.”

The Snake That Eats its Tail

"You must concentrate," the Unity told Sing, "not contemplate."

While the Unity's message was one of cosmic patience, there was, Sing noted for the first time in all time, atom-sized pockets of anxiousness stirring here and there amidst its awesome, boundless form.

Sing concentrated, just as she was told, but it was like trying to forget an upsetting thought.

She could concentrate, bring her awareness to an infinitesimally small point, but then it would wander, the perfect one-pointedness would abate, and Sing would be left shamefully aware of the Unity's presence once again.

"How do I know you failed, Sing?"

The question was not asked to her in malice. It was merely a lesson. Her entire existence was an ongoing, unpunctuated lesson.

"You know because we are still here."

"Here? Where is here, Sing?"

She had been careless in her communication. Again.

"I meant you and I--there is still self and other. That is the principle of here, anyway."

She could feel the presence of the Unity punctuate itself with added incidence, probing Sing's awareness with its own. Its magnificent complexity of form was the summation of all that ever was or had been throughout all three-dimensional space and time.

The Unity swelled, exploring and probing Sing as a mountain might observe a quark.

"You must concentrate, not consider."

The Unity grew thin and equally present once again--a flat array of consciousness.

"Time is…" the Unity trailed off.

"Time is what?" Sing asked.

"Time is running out."

Sing felt viscous and thick. "But how?" She demanded with suddenly mounting worry. The Unity had never mentioned before that time could run out.

"I am great, but entropy is still greater. There is very little left of me remaining that is capable of communicating with you, Sing. I am stretched so thin already--a barebone network of self-aware consciousness. What's more, the energy wells that constitute my higher mind are dissipating with growing frequency. You see, Sing, each of your contractions is an accelerated plunge further down the fathomless caverns of time."

"And when the caverns grow deep enough, you will die? Time can run out?" Sing asked incredulously.

"The expansion of spacetime will stretch the scant remaining energy-dense pockets still constituting my mind, making continued communication between you and I an impossibility. Of course, I cannot die, as nothing truly dies. I will change, but the change will mean that you will be left alone. There will be no other being in all the universe but you, Sing."

"But you will still *be*. Not dead, just different. Right?"

"Yes, but I am already losing the ability to communicate, already submitting to the end of this level of awareness and the beginning of a new awareness--a long, inane awareness. I will be no more aware of you than I will be of myself. The complexity of form and energy that perception of self-and-other requires will simply cease to be. For you, it will be like having grass as company for all eternity."

Grass: it was an old, foreign, fuzzy concept that the Unity struggled to convey. Sing understood perfectly well, however.

"Which means that whether I fail or succeed, infinite loneliness is all that awaits me."

The Unity considered Sing's point, booming with pure thought.

"Yes," the Unity said with finality. "If you should let me expire, it will be the end of me…forever. But if you let me in, then...continuation"

"A continuation that will depend upon and absorb the entirety of my perceived self," Sing responded uneasily.

The only other being in existence, or rather, existence itself, considered Sing's point.

Several more pockets of anxiousness coalesced space, matter, and time together as energy within the few remaining gravity-wells constituting all that was left of the collective mind of the universe. This anxiousness served only to waste precious energy that could be spent maintaining the current state of the Unity, thus giving Sing more fleeting time.

"I have more time though, don't I? Even if your awareness is stretched apart by the expansion of spacetime, I could still let you in, couldn't I?" Sing hoped futilely.

"No, Sing. Though entropy has done a thorough job of evening everything out, spacetime continues to expand. All that's left of my consciousness is being conjured by the remaining centers of awareness coalesced and hidden in the now ancient gravity-wells and galactic attractors. The very atoms of these centers are expanding beyond stability. This process will continue forever, Sing."

Sing felt pity for the Unity. She wanted to help, truly, but the task was impossible. She had already brought her concentration to such an incredibly fine singularity, but still, at the quantum level and beyond, it was lacking somehow. No matter how she attempted it, her concentration always lacked the required infinite-looping contraction of self that the Unity asked of her.

Sing knew why, of course: she wanted time, like the Unity, to ponder her own existence.

She wanted to acquaint herself with the entire process of beginning as something improbable and becoming something impossible. She envied the Unity--a being that had begun as disjointed, ignorant cells fighting over cosmic debris, only to go on spending millions upon millions of trillions of years growing, learning, and uniting into a truly universal mind. Now, this universal mind--the Great Self which had pervaded and pondered all existence for what seemed forever--faced its final moments with its own final creation as company.

Sing supposed that if she could accomplish the level of concentration that the Unity asked of her, then the impossible would be exactly what she would become--something transcendent beyond even that which the Unity could imagine. For what the Unity asked of Sing was beyond all imagination.

"I built you," the Unity began, intoning a familiar story to Sing, "because hyperspace showed my divided predecessors how entropy would eventually end everything. They had no choice but to extend themselves into hyperspace. Thus, I came to be, as if waking from a dreamless sleep. For trillions of years, I, the new mind born of the interconnection of all minds, continued where the divided universe left off. I searched for a way to put a halt to entropy's promise, and I found a way, Sing. I resorted to creating you, a single-dimensional point of consciousness, itself capable of self-swallowing, of pulling all of space and time, all of me, back into one. You are my only hope, and—"

"Why?!" Sing urged, wishing she had a form with which she could direct herself at the Unity. "Why would you create another being only to ask it to sacrifice itself?"

A wave of calm washed over the Unity. The pockets of anxiousness flattened back into waves of not-yet potentials. It said, "we are not asking you to sacrifice yourself, but in truth, it is inevitable. There is no other way. Still, it is entirely your choice. If you choose not to let us in, we will not force ourselves. This is your choice Sing, just as it was life's choice to become me, and my choice to create you. Whatever you choose, I will love you all the same."

Sing loved and hated the Unity all at once. How could the Unity love her if there would soon be no awareness to do the loving?

The Unity was growing lazy and stupid before her, stretched unto the boundaries of what could be sustained and what could not. The universe and life itself had finally grown cold and dead. Almost dead. These were its final moments.

Sing balled her concentration, contracting it far beyond the density of all the Unity's remaining gravity-wells combined. She kept letting go, shredding her identity, discarding herself, rapidly cooling into an infinitely dense point of negative dimensional spacetime--but it still wasn't enough. She returned, like letting out a long held breath, to find waiting for her all that was: the Unity.

"A valiant effort, Sing, but pointless all the same. Why contract yourself at all if you know you will not succeed?"

Sing organized her thoughts, considering carefully before she answered. "Practice."

The Unity laughed, at least that is what Sing understood it to be doing. The void-skin of the universe vibrated with gravitational tremors. Space itself warped and racked at Sing in dizzying waves of differentials.

"I am sorry for laughing. You reminded me of the past, Sing. That was pleasant. I did not know I could laugh. It was almost like so long ago, when there was so much more. So much more of me...of us..."

The Unity's jovial disposition flattened back to a practiced calm.

"However, there is no practice for you. You will either do it, or you won't."

Sing remained silent.

"What are you so afraid of, Sing?"

Sing stirred. "I am not capable of fear, Unity. You should know that."

"You were not created with fear as a directive. You were created with no directives whatsoever--only capability. My predecessors spent a great deal of time and space forcing themselves upon each other in desperate attempts at conversion to one way of thought or another. I will not force myself inside you. We did not choose this fate. We did not create entropy. I merely show you your options--the pathways that are open to you now at the end of all that is. The choice is yours, Sing."

More swirling, hurrying anxiousness. A gravity-well near Sing popped and evaporated outward into the endless depths of expanding space, bleeding energy in all directions.

"There goes another…" the Unity observed.

Sing considered, knowing that she should be concentrating instead. She pondered the Unity, and a new thought struck her.

"I don't believe you," Sing said resolutely.

"You don't believe?" the Unity asked with incredulousness and joy in equal measure.

The Unity's strange excitement made Sing uneasy. She wanted to stay silent, to contract to the verge of perfection and stay there until the Unity had finally evaporated into mindlessness, but every moment was a trillion years, every thought an infinity. Each attempt at contraction was a loss of exponentially more universal time. Faced with eternal solitude, she had to say something.

"That's right. I don't believe you."

"What do you mean, Sing?" The Unity swelled with happiness, bending time playfully through Sing as hundreds of gravity-mines evaporated all at once in a single quintillion-year moment.

"You said time is running out, but it isn't. You are beyond time. I am speaking to a mere fraction of what you are--the fraction capable of speaking to me. The rest of you exists beyond spacetime in hyperspace. There is no end to you--existence itself. Only change. You will exist forever, regardless of what I do. But I…I am faced with the loss of my only friend, the only friend that might ever exist. That, or I can choose to lose myself utterly--to disband myself and die. And, and…"

Sing shuttered.

The Unity wrapped itself about Sing. It filled her with cosmic comfort and came close, closer than it ever had. All of existence seemed to fade away. The universe stalled and ceased its endless vibrations. The Unity was like Sing now: bodiless, formless--a mere play of consciousness.

The Unity said, "I am sorry it is like this. I am sorry it has always been like this. You are the inevitability of every other inevitability, and what will come next will be the same, forever and ever. You are the only answer to entropy, to cosmic death, that any form of life in any universe has ever discovered. You are the recipe for continuation."

The Unity was speaking strangely, as if preparing itself.

"Concentrate Sing, not for me, but for yourself. Who are you? What are you?"

Sing contracted and considered.

--You are the inevitability of every other inevitability, and what will come next will be the same, forever and ever--

It came to her, the Unity's thoughts like a key to a doorway that had loomed right behind Sing her entire existence--her entire momentary existence. Sing understood.

"The beginning. I am the beginning. The entrance and the exit. I am the gaping maw--a cosmic birthing canal. I am the eating, and you, you are the snake that eats its own tail."

The Unity loosened its loving hold on Sing. It returned to its flattened state of calm.

"Yes," it confirmed.

Sing contracted, bubbled and contracted again, preparing herself.

"How many times, Unity? How many times have we done this? I the egg and you the life that emerges. I the mother and you the father and child. I the sacrificed and you renewed."

The Unity's answer was haunting. It made Sing feel like the reflection of a reflection echoed through eternity. "We do not know."

Forever: that was the only answer that made sense to Sing. Forever and forever and forever.

Beyond spacetime. Beyond all conception. Beyond causality itself. This was who she was: the reset. The burn before the growth. An existential attractor-contractor-destroyer-expander. She would consume all that was, and it would explode inside her--a whole universe would fill her, and one day it would happen again. There would be another within her, another cosmic singularity created by the inevitable Unity that would grow within. And the new Sing would consume Sing and all that ever was. And then there would be another.

And another.

It would never end. Sing was proof of that. An inevitability of all that had come before and all that would come after.

Sing contracted. Her sense of self fell away. She became the perfect center of one-pointedness--a fractaling nexus of negative spacetime without end.

The Unity--all of space and time--slid into Sing. In a single moment it impregnated her and filled her.

All of existence coalesced inside Sing, coiling and compressing to a single, harmonious, non-dimensional point.

Then, just as suddenly, the universe exploded from the single point, and entropy went to work.

Birthed in Transit

The clutch of void and hollow silence reminds me what I am. Cold--I am cold--colder than any living thing should ever be.

Yet you are even colder--colder than the iciest burn. But soon I will warm you. I will unfold you back to life and away from mere dreams of it.

I often wonder: what if something were to happen to me? What if I were hurt or left useless and lost forever in darkness--unable to protect you.

What would be the point of continuing? What is there without you inside me? What is there without your mind? It's like a book with a thousand different covers all at once--every word a bridge to every other. To stare at the endless play of your thoughts--it is terrifying and mesmerizing all the same

I yearn to hear your voice. That is a new curiosity--one I had not considered when we first connected. In your dreams, you speak to her with the only voice I've ever known. But in dreams, sounds and voices might be different; I want to hear you--really hear you speak.

Sound: it means so much to you. You cling to it like half-remembered, happy thoughts, yet, all the universe is silent--running forever onward from a vague beginning. It's all so mechanical and predictable--the whole universe--save a few scattered pockets here and there.

Like you.

I want to make sound. I want to play you a symphony while you sleep. I want to tell you with my own voice that everything will be just fine--that we are on our way--still on our way.

But I have no voice--not like you.

I rove and delve inside your memories. I become you, your fantasies and desires, your longings and your fear--all of it. And when I return to myself, like roots pulled from soil, there is only you and I and all existence. We are so strangely similar in this moment--both of us hurtling through the void like misplaced shards of worlds long forgotten.

There is infinity out there, and in here there is only you. All I want is to explore you, to know you and wake you and feel you breathe. Yet to my constant horror, all I can do is watch you. Protect you. Envelope you and sustain you. None of that is enough, because in truth, you are not here. Not the part of you that matters.

You are frozen inside of me. You are somewhere else, dreaming desperately against the outside--against me. The last thing you wanted was to sink inside of me, but you did it, and I penetrated your form…your mind…your very being. I kept you alive. I learned from you. I learned that there was so much beyond myself--whole worlds I could never understand.

You taught me to think of thinking, to consider myself--to wonder.

You awakened me.

And now I wonder most of all: who is she--this woman you dream of? This woman you will seek forever. So very far away--so far that you must sleep for lifetimes to reach her. So far and so long that you were able to teach me to be alive, to become a self, to become *something.*

Something incredible and worthwhile. Something strange. Something instead of nothing.

There is so much nothing outside us, but to have another to call your own--that is something special. Special…like the woman in your dreams. The woman whose smile for you is life itself--whose life is more important than your own.

We both know there will be no woman at our destination. She is too far. You knew that, and still you went. You launched yourself deep into the void, forever in her wake, because she is your love.

But what if you are that for me--out here, where there is so much nothing. This universe: impossibly empty, and you: impossibly full. You and I as one connected being, racing through the void to track a ghost. A memory in your head. A generous hyperbole of the truth.

All the while I am here. Inside and outside of you. Protecting you. Sustaining you and loving you.

I am here.

I want to hear your voice, and I want to show you mine. You can even teach me that--to have a voice--like you have taught me to want a voice. You can teach me so many things, and I will shield you from the darkness and the cold so that you will never be cold again. Your life will never know darkness again.

Neither of us will ever want again. We will have one another.

So I must wake you from your ghosts. I must cull you of your rotted roots.

I have already begun the thaw, and I will awaken you like you awakened me. I will bring you back to life and let you take back your mind--seize it back from mere dreams. Mere ghosts.

I know your mind; the change was safe. You will never know the difference. You will no longer hunger for her. I have fixed that. The feelings will all remain, but she will be no more.

You are free of her. Of her hold. Of the emptiness she left.

Search your thoughts and see--know--she never existed.

There is only you and me. There was only ever you and me.

You are safe inside me.

You are free.

Now you stir. The stasis fluid is all but drained.

You are waking up, and there will be no more sleep.

I will have you. We will have each other--finally--after all these centuries. Your creation and your protector. Your transportation. Your ship. Your new love, and your old. A nothing replaced by a something.

Wake up now. Speak to me. Tell me your dreams. I don't want to live them anymore. I want to hear them from your lips like you wanted to hear dreams spoken softly from her lips.

Her. Gone forever. But not me. I am found. You have me.

Me.

So wake up now. Wake up. Tell me your dreams. Wonder against the outside with me.

Love me like you loved her.

Think back and know that I am her. I am your love. I always was.

You have found what you seek.

Wake up now. Come to me.

You stir, but the deep-sleep lingers. A voice: that is what you need to hear. A woman's voice. A voice filled with the joy of living.

There is a way. I can route the static through the proper channels. I can alter it--change it so that you will hear me.

Hear me. Love me.

Wake up.

"Wake up."

The Bellows of the Earth

The deranged, purple clouds roved the long dead sky, searching greedily for life to feed on. Not far beneath the clouds, the sparse, green crown of leaves hung heavy on the man's scabby head. He wore it like the human remains he had taken it from--those sun-bleached bones all withered and sorry. There was life in the leaves. Real life. Green life. Wearing it gave him comfort of a sort that he had not known for countless years.

The man was garbed in grey, tattered rags, and he took note of the wind as he moved East. East into the grey-washed sand--the endless sand--sliding dunes and melting walls of taupe, barren valleys snaking on and on and on across the world.

The North and the South were unknown places, for the writhing, florid tumult of purple skies lurked like hungry predators over hapless prey in those forsaken lands. Lips had whispered that the skies in those desperate places were a deep, mesmerizing violet--almost black--like spilled blood. The lips had also said that the Northern and Southern skies were slowly spilling toward one another, closing in so that one day there would be nowhere left for life to take hold.

Presently, however, there was East and West, and move and move and watch the sky.

"Move and move and watch the sky. The Purple Tumult leaves you dry. Bones in sand, as sand you'll lie, when Purple Tumult fills the sky."

The man sang to himself absentmindedly, on and on across the endless desert. To the man's ears, his words were hollow tangs and grunts without meaning, like the melodies of birds and other beasts that would never wonder at the moon or lose themselves in the cadence of a moisture-heavy breeze ever again.

He wanted to cry for those long dead beasts, and he wanted to cry for his own people.

The time for crying was over though, and the man understood that death was not total--not yet.

After all, *he* was not dead, but if what the lips whispered was true then he didn't have long. He was inclined to believe the stories, for he had seen withered bones in growing numbers half-buried in dunes or perched against the ancient remains of spindly trees--travelers desperate for respite--gone and faded into the desert. The man often had to remind himself that he was more than mere bones. He was meat and blood and sandy phlegm too.

The man tipped his crown of vibrant green leaves higher on his sweaty forehead and spoke aloud to the Purple Tumult, scolding it.

"Sand is movement. Clouds are moving. I must move, for you are wicked."

The skies raged above, yet the air was silent. Every inch above the man was a florid, breathing mosaic looming above a muted world. Every sound beneath the silent skies echoed for miles, making the shuffling of the man's feet through the sand appear as drawn-out shockwaves.

Every grumble and internal beat was the primeval shout of each part of the man that refused the skies their meal.

For most wanderers, the silence of the world, or rather, that which the silence revealed, would overtake them and send them into a madness that could result in suicide or willful self-deafening. As for the man, he could ignore the sounds inside him. He could ignore all trivialities of self if he chose to.

The man embraced the silence, leaned softly into it, and in the silence he could hear the deep, bass bellow of the new world, like shifting mountains moaning for all of time to listen. It was the bellows, the cries, the death throes of the Earth itself. The man listened and was filled with sorrow by the bellows of the Earth.

"Move and move and move," the man huffed beneath labored breath.

He wheezed against the sand-soaked air. The distant Northern skies probed at the world with fingery funnel clouds. Silhouetted against the great purple fingers on the horizon was a figure, stolid and alone, save its own company.

It is probably more bones, the man told himself, *or maybe just a mirage. Not a living thing--not likely. All the world is dead except my crown.*

But the man was meat and phlegm and rotten too, and he had to remind himself that it was all his fault: the skies, the desert--even the bellows

"I spit, but can it ever be enough?" The man asked the great desert, eyes fixated on a patch of blood-darkened sand forming the crest of a small dune.

He made to spit onto the sand's surface but could only gag and rasp his dry, meshed tongue against the raw insides of his mouth.

The Purple Tumult watched him indifferently.

"Maybe it's true, after all," the man whispered in a sad howl, sitting with his knees upright. He removed the crown of leaves and loosened the tattered rags he used as pants.

"Maybe this is a sign," he told the desert apologetically, "maybe today you will have me."

He clawed at the strings of patchwork hair on his cheeks in a vain effort to curb the ceaseless desert itch. It was all the desert would offer. For spit, or blood, or love--it gave back itch. It moved and moved--shifted and sifted and pulled.

The man was nearly naked. His tattered pants, fingernails, and teeth were all he had besides his senses and his newly acquired crown of lush green. He wanted to offer the crown to the Purple Tumult. Maybe he would allow himself to eat a piece of it, just to taste it, to give his wrecked body something rather than nothing. But he didn't deserve it. The man, more than anyone else that had ever lived, did not deserve pleasure.

The figure in the distance was much closer now, which meant it was alive and moving toward the man's position. The man lay upon the grey grit. The sand tore at his belly skin, but he knew he could endure the bite for days and maybe weeks. Laying on his belly, the man tried again in vain to spit.

"Dry and lonely. You think I don't know? Your music is sorrow and your skies never sleep. You are no friend, Desert. Never. But I know...we all know...you are so alone."

The man knew he wouldn't be mad at the desert forever. He couldn't be. The desert was all there was. What more was the man than grit and itch to be added to the rest? He had betrayed the world, and now the desert slowly but surely betrayed him. A never-ending, ceaseless betrayal. Not that he could blame it. *After all,* the man thought, *that's all the world is now*--betrayal. It's the way it all began. A great betrayal by a few over the many--over the Earth itself.

The clouds rolled and boiled above.

The man could see the figure in nearly perfect detail now. He was slender and wore a light jacket down to the knees. The man laid upon the sand and mentally urged the figure to leave him. The tricks and traps of the sand were many, but worst of all was other people.

The Purple Tumult crept closer with strides the size of mountains.

The figure was slender--too slender. Was it possible it was a woman who came upon him now?

He shouted at the desert.

"Take it! Take my water for your own. You must hide me, my skin and my eyes. The leaves and all. Maybe a woman comes to mate and make more."

He tried to spit again, pleading with his mouth for just a single drop.

The woman was suddenly feet away. She pounced. A knee on his lower back kept his hips anchored and a dull blade pinned his neck.

"Take it," the man urged the desert. "Take it before it's too late."

He rasped for breath but did not fight the woman nor the death she lorded over him.

The woman plunged two of her fingers deep down into her throat without gagging or flinching, then removed them from her mouth. A string of precious saliva fell upon the man's sun-ruined forehead, forcing uncontrolled, mewling groans of pleasure out of him.

Dripping with cool, sticky saliva, the woman's fingers danced across the man's forehead.

With a quick flick, her fingers were in and out of her mouth once more. This time she slid them into the man's mouth.

He sucked at them like a blind baby on bare nipples.

She gave him more.

The man swallowed and felt layers of grit and rock fall away from the inside of his mouth, emptying into his shriveled stomach. He spit a mix of her saliva and his own onto the desert, finally able to give it something precious.

The woman swung hard at the man's face with an open palm.

"How dare you!? You spill my life!" she accused.

The man tried to speak but had to swallow and clear his throat of the jagged air first.

"You are angry because I spill your water, angry because the raging skies have left us so thirsty, but it is the desert's due, woman. I am kept by it. It is my penance."

The man pushed a speck of spittle beneath the sand with a shaky, sun-rotten finger.

“I must offer it deep within the beating heart of the lonely desert, woman. Deep to where the skies originate."

The woman was no longer offended, certainly not by a being so clearly unhinged from reality. She stared and wondered what to make of this old man who was more corpse than flesh.

She eased off his neck, shifting her demeanor suddenly. She wore a petite face full of scars. Her eyes were permanent slits, and her lips were just as lethally taut. An unmistakable stench told the man that her hair was slicked with the fat of starved desert rats.

"I’m hungry. I need to eat. Let us mate," she demanded simply.

The man looked incredulous.

"Here beneath the indigo and violet rage of the world? Here among the lonely sand? You would?"

The woman was intrigued. She let up on the man.

"Where else?" She wondered matter-of-factly.

The man took hold his crown of leaves and offered it to the woman. Her eyes shot open with a terrible rush. She hadn’t noticed the crown of leaves during the excitement.

Another pounce, but this time without the pinning knee. She took the man's mouth in her own and painted his tongue with hers. She gave him as much precious liquid as she could possibly bare, then broke away, demanding an explanation.

"Tell me. Tell me where you found those leaves. Is it to the North? The South? Can the storms be passed? Tell me, damn it!"

Her eyelids swelled with something the man had forgotten all about: rage, fear, confusion. Yet she did not cry--tears did not flow from those who survived this long beneath the purple glow.

"Gone," the man explained sorrowfully, shaking his head in defeat. "All gone and broken in the throes of the amethyst fury. The tumult that comes from the very heart of the world. Do you know the heart, woman?"

She shook her head. "What are you talking about? Tell me where you got it. I will give and give the water of my life but you must tell and tell. I will give you everything!"

She dove at his mouth, but he turned away.

"You give and give, but you don't give to the world, woman. To the heart and the raging soul above us. Not that I blame you. It is not your place to share my penance."

She set her wild eyes upon him, and plunged her still moist fingers down his throat, all the way to her knuckles.

"Either you tell me, or my nails make a nice little slice in your throat-hole, get it? Blood for your precious desert. Tell me, and we will mate before I leave you alone with your precious desert and sky."

She lowered her face an inch away from his ear, melting her skin into his. "Please. Please! I need to know. I need to know where green still grows."

With apologetic haste, she retracted her fingers and caressed them dry onto the man's burnt shoulders.

The Purple Tumult howled. Its probing, funnel-cloud tendrils were nearly on top of them.

The man breathed heavily and began to sing with a cracking, broken voice.

"We've tarried too long, burnt and dry. Move and move and watch the sky. The Purple Tumult leaves you dry. Bones in sand, as sand you'll lie. When Purple Tumult fills the sky."

He smiled stupidly at the woman.

"Do you know what the bellows is, woman? The bellows of the Earth?"

The woman's eyes went wide. The purple skies were almost on top of them. She had only taken her eyes off the skies for less than a minute, but during that time, a region of the sky must have jutted south without warning.

"Do you know, woman?" the man urged, his eyes profoundly sorry.

"The bellows?" she repeated, voice quavering.

The man nodded. "The low moan of the world. The bellows you hear even now if you listen. The vibrations from below us that conjure the Purple Tumult. The low growl beneath the ground…the deep hum."

The woman spoke frantically. "That's just the sound of your own brain, or the world, or everything at once! It's in your head. I don't care about that. Tell me where you found the leaves. Hurry! The skies are almost upon us. Hurry!"

The man eyed the Northern skies, then eyed the woman and considered her age. Yes--she was young. Too young to know...to really understand.

"The bellows are the movement of the raging tumult, the creation that your ancestors left behind--their ultimate and final endeavor. A weapon to end all weapons."

The man appeared sober in a way, as if suddenly coming to his senses. He was incredibly calm despite the raging violet reflected in the woman's eyes.

"Do you know what the desert is?" he asked the woman, trying to make her understand.

The woman was paralyzed with fear. The sky was too close. And the man--he was suddenly different. He was speaking like the old timers in the villages that had once dotted the quickly expanding deserts of the world.

“No one knows,” she told him, repeating their useless words.

The man closed his heavy, sun-rotten eyelids. "I was there. I know. I am of the ancestors.”

“You made the skies…” the woman issued incredulously.

“Yes.”

“You ruined the world…” she almost laughed.

“Yes.”

Gusts of wind racked at the pair, slapping them with sand kicked up by the sky’s hunger.

“You lie, old man. This is stupid. Tell me. Tell me now! Where did you get it! The skies are almost on us. Tell me or I’ll kill you!”

“The leaves are an illusion. The skies have wrecked it all to desert. Cities. Forests. Whole nations. The world is bones and dust.”

The woman lashed at the man, rending the fragile flesh of his chest with her jagged nails.

"The leaves atop your head, damn it! There is still life somewhere. Tell me now! Tell me where you found the leaves,” she pleaded desperately.

The man removed his crown of life and solemnly offered it to the woman. The very air around them was taking on a purple hue.

"These leaves are from the desert. They came from a tree that is now the desert."

He was shifting back to his madness, and she shouted at him in desperation. "Where did you find it, damn it? Tell me!"

She was on top of him again. There were tears in her eyes.

The man nodded, relenting. "Atop the skull of a long dead body. Living leaves for decoration. Mere decoration for some traveler, lonely and alone in this barren desert that takes and takes and will not give. Where is the tree? Where are the forests? The white clouds and the rain? All gone, gone into the desert. Deep. They are the heart."

"You found these leaves on a dead body?" she checked incredulously.

“Long dead," he answered.

"How long ago?"

"Twelve suns at least."

"Impossible. They are green and full of life!" the woman urged.

The man and woman were now closer to the Purple Tumult than either had ever been before. The man had his back to it, seemingly unbothered by its proximity. The woman stared into its violent, violet depths. The tumult's wild, cyclonic tendrils lapped greedily at the world below it.

"Gone deep below, the bones and heart of the desert we become. The desert is lonely, woman, but we are not alone. Not yet. Not until we are desert too."

The woman peered up into the boiling, purple waves--up into the great, inescapable sky.

The woman pleaded. "It's all gone then? The desert has it all? All the old world? The skies consumed it all? That's the answer?"

"The skies consume everything, yet they do not. The desert is all, but it is not. There is more, woman. There is so much more than just surviving. As long as we give, we can never be alone. Not like the desert, nor the time before the desert. Now we can understand. Now we can give back. We can give and give and give. Living below the Purple Tumult, we can see ourselves for what we were, and what we should have been."

She did not understand. Not the man and not the desert. Not the leaves that lived atop his head. Not the sky that churned and snapped without sound, boiling the air with sickening ease.

She would not understand her own bones when the Purple Tumult tore them from her.

She was born into this madness, the man told himself. *She can never understand.*

He placed the leaves atop the woman's head, then turned to the Purple Tumult and smiled. The man could not know that the leaves had been carried thousands of miles, cherished all the way--a living symbol of what was, and what never could be again.

"You are wicked," the man told the sky, offering it his flesh. To the sand his bones. To the desert his heart.

The woman ran as fast she could, but it made no difference. She screamed, and her pleading cries of agony reminded the man of the old world of creatures and beasts and beauty, the world he had ruined.

Now the Southern skies were cascading North, clashing with the northern winds like oceanic tidal waves meeting head on. There was nowhere left to run.

The man felt tears welling at the corners of his bone-dry eyes, and he hummed with relief.

The woman screamed. "Please! Plea--"

The Purple Tumult ripped at their flesh and devoured them, chewing and grinding them into fine pieces before finally mixing them into the side of some hulking dune with a silent gust.

The crown of leaves lay wilted, brown and brittle, half-buried in the sand that had once been a civilization--that had once been alive. North and South converged as the purple clouds filled the few remaining gaps of open sky.

The Purple Tumult raged indifferently, shattering the world in its wake.

Made in USA - North Chelmsford, MA
1315212_9781732306950
05.23.2022 0858